Praise for *Eartheater*

"A raw and vital literary debut, *Eartheater* takes an unwavering and visceral look at systems of power through the perspective of a young woman caught in the crosshairs."
—*Shelf Awareness*

"In Reyes's hands, this coming-of-age novel flowers into a meditation on death, and the earth all children will eat in the end."
—*The Observer*

"Reyes succeeds in making the feisty Eartheater and her visions both persuasive and affecting."
—*Library Journal* (starred review)

"A rising star of Argentine lit offers a provocatively offbeat coming-of-age story about a teen girl with the ability to solve crimes by ingesting the dirt on which the newly dead or missing once walked."
—*O, the Oprah Magazine*

"A stirring genre blend of fantasy and crime fiction that combines graceful prose and magic realism."
—*Booklist* (starred review)

"Reyes's coming-of-age portrait stands out for her unflinching look at a teen's exploration of sex and death."
—*Publishers Weekly*

"Compelling and visceral, Reyes' debut combines mystery and coming-of-age to evoke the stories of the victims of femicide."
—*Kirkus Reviews*

Eartheater

A Novel

Dolores Reyes

Translated from the Spanish
by Julia Sanches

HARPERVIA
An Imprint of HarperCollins*Publishers*

HarperCollins books may be purchased for educational, business, or sales promotional use. For information, please email the Special Markets Department at SPsales@harpercollins.com.

Originally published as *Cometierra* in Argentina in 2019 by Sigilo Editorial.

Translation Copyright © 2020 by Julia Sanches.

FIRST HARPERCOLLINS PAPERBACK EDITION PUBLISHED IN 2021

Designed by SBI Book Arts, LLC

Library of Congress Cataloging-in-Publication Data is available upon request.

ISBN 978-0-06-298775-4

21 22 23 24 25   LSC   10 9 8 7 6 5 4 3 2 1

In memory of Melina Romero and Araceli Ramos.
For the victims of femicide, for its survivors.

you who have only sweet words for the dead

LEOPOLDO MARIA PANERO

No one has yet determined what the body can do.

BARUCH SPINOZA (AS TRANSLATED BY EDWIN CURLEY)

The dead don't hang near the living. Get it through your head."

"I don't care. Mamá stays here. In my house. In the earth."

"Drop it already. Everybody's waiting."

When they don't listen, I scarf earth.

I used to do it for me, for the fuss, because it annoyed and embarrassed them. The earth was dirty, they said, my belly would bloat like a toad.

"Get up already. Scrub up a little."

Then, I started eating earth for others who wanted to speak. Others, already gone.

"What do you think graveyards are for? For burying people, that's what. Now get dressed."

"I don't care about people. Mamá is mine. Mamá stays here."

"You look like a wild thing. You haven't even brushed your hair."

I gaze at the room, at the wooden walls Mamá had wanted to line with bricks on the inside. The sheet metal roof, real tall and gray. The floor, my bed, and the part of the room where she lay down to sleep whenever the old man got nasty.

It'll be empty over there, I think, then bury my head in a pillow. Mamá used to brush me, Mamá used to cut my hair.

"You want to be dragged kicking and screaming? Don't be a brat. You ought to be ashamed, making a stink on a day like this."

I spring up. My hair covers nearly my whole tank top, a curtain that brushes my panties. I crouch. I look around for my sneakers and for yesterday's pants, probably on the floor somewhere. And I keep my tears to myself, so all that's left is a fury that seizes me like a spasm.

To get to the bathroom I have to leave my room and pass people swarming my house like flies. Mouthy neighbors who smoke and chatter.

Walter must've gone on strike. Nobody forces his hand.

No more Mamá and me.

I pull on a pair of pants, tuck in my top. I do up the button then the zipper, my eyes fixed on Tía. Maybe she'll lay off me a while.

I get up. I leave the room and walk behind those hands carting a shrouded body, 'cause I've had enough. 'Cause I want them to leave already.

Walter doesn't want to come.

To watch her fall quietly into a gaping pit in the graveyard, in the back, where they bury the poor. With no tombstones, or plaques. A parched mouth that devours her near the reedbed. The earth, open like a wound. And there I am, trying to stop her, with the strength of my arms, with this body that can't even cover the span of that hole. Mamá falls anyhow.

My strength, slight, makes no difference.

The earth swaddles her like the old man's blows and I'm glued to the ground, as ever near this body being taken from me like it's a burglary.

Meanwhile, voices pray.

For what? In the end, only the earth's stirred up.

No more Mamá and me, not anymore.

In she goes. They cover her. I gawk, ear to earth. I can still breathe. I didn't think I'd manage, I thought my ribs would've caved in and scraped at my lungs.

The sound of this place lives on in my nightmares, a waste of pestilence and pain.

Even the sun baffles me, bleeding onto my hot skin. My eyes sting like somebody threw acid on me, and blink back tears.

Pain: the yellow of garbage, of fever; or gray, sheet-metal-gray, sickness-gray. Only pain seems never to die.

They're going to leave you here, Mamá, all of them, even though I don't want them to. Even though my hands won't let them, you're going to stay.

There isn't much I can do to stop the earth from being the enemy, except eat it. This strange earth I've taken from a graveyard neither of us ever stepped foot in.

She'll stay here and I'll carry some of this earth inside me. So that, in the dark, I can know my dreams.

I shut my eyes to lay hands on the fresh earth covering you, Mamá, and night falls. I make fists, scoop, bring it to my mouth. The earth devouring you is dark and tastes like tree bark. It pleases me and reveals things and makes me see.

Is it dawning? No. It's the sun scorching my eyes and skin. I think the earth is poisoning me.

They say:

"Up, Eartheater, get up already. Let go of her. Let her go."

But I keep my eyes closed. I fight the repulsion to eat more earth. I can't, I won't leave without seeing, without knowing.

Someone says:

"Too broke for a box?"

And forces me to open my eyes.

Mamá, you're falling into a hole wrapped in a shroud that's more or less a rag. Who'll talk to me now? I'm nothing without you, and I don't want to be. Will the earth talk? It already has:

They beat her. I see the blows but can't feel them. The fury of fists pounding holes in flesh. I see Papá, hands like my hands, arms strong for fists, snagging your heart and your flesh like a fishhook. And something, like a river, beginning to run.

To die, Mamá, and carve you afresh from the both of us.

"Up, Eartheater, get up already. Let go of her. Let her go."

Part One

Part One

Walter was good, unlike Tía. He'd sit on my bed and listen, rarely talk. He wouldn't get angry if I grabbed a pillow and slept on the floor from time to time, beneath his bed, the wood slats and his mattress the ceiling of a house all my body's. He'd stay with me, for hours. Waiting.

I listened to the noises around the house. I grew.

Sometimes my brother would ask about Papá. "The old man," he'd say. He wanted to know if he'd come by, if I'd bumped into him again.

"I don't know anything about him. Should I ask the earth?"

"No," Walter always said, "it'll hurt you."

One afternoon I waited for Tía to go buy some food and snuck out. I looked for Walter in the next room. They'd taken out the big bed.

I'm all on my own, I thought. *What if Walter and Tía never come home?*

3

I went to the kitchen and opened a can of peas. Not wanting to waste them, I emptied the can over the table. A slimy liquid oozed from the pea mound in the middle. I felt like eating them but didn't. My tummy needed to be empty. I went looking for a knife and, opening the drawer, spotted my old man's bottle opener.

I needed something of his so that I could ask the earth about him, but Walter and Tía had been busy rubbing him out of the house, and out of my life. They'd even got rid of his bed. I grabbed the bottle opener from the drawer and studied it. Then, as happy as if I'd found a treasure, I stuffed it in my shorts pocket.

I walked out of the house, barefoot, hair hanging loose, bottle opener in my pocket, empty can in one hand and knife in the other.

I sat on our land, ran my hand over the earth, rammed the knife in the ground and pulled it out. I liked it. I stabbed again. This time I didn't pull out the knife but tried to shimmy it, to get the earth to crack open and loosen up a bit. Though the earth was strong, it still let me. Once it started to give, I put my hand down and closed it. Earth in fist. I set the soil on my shorts. I collected it there. Meanwhile, I used the knife and my hand to loosen the earth. Then, I took my old man's bottle opener from my pocket and placed it in the hole. Upright, smack in the middle. Fistful by fistful, I covered it with earth until it was completely buried. I wiped my hands on my shorts and legs.

Seated, my hair reached the floor and was the color of the ground I lived on.

I wanted something to crawl out of there, even a critter would do, but I got nothing. Even so, I waited, staring down at my hands, my legs, the knife. Then, I gathered everything up—the earth, the bottle opener—and thought of the last time I'd seen my old man crack open a bottle of beer.

It hurt to think of. Miffed, I shoved everything in the can.

I stood up and walked inside. A bit of pea juice had dribbled onto the floor. I pulled up a chair and sat down. In one hand I held the can while the other lay open, palm up. I tried to pour a small amount of dirt into my open hand but everything came tumbling out, both earth and bottle opener. Dirt spilled on the floor. I brought the rest to my mouth and ate it, hungry to see Papá again. I coated my tongue, closed my mouth, tried to swallow. The earth felt like it had gone from being a thing in my hand to something alive. Loving earth inside me. I kept on eating. Once I ran out of dirt, I turned to the bottle opener. Licked it clean.

Belly heavy with earth, I shut my eyes.

"Papá's alive," I later said to Walter and Tía, when I saw them gawking at me. I thought they'd be happy, but I was wrong. They were quiet. Like, frozen still. I ran up to Walter and hugged him.

"What the fuck have you done, you twerp?" my tía said, grabbing my arm to pull me away from my brother.

"Walter, Papá's alive," I repeated as she yanked me back.

My brother came to me again and grabbed my hand. He took me to the bathroom and scrubbed my legs with a sponge, then left the faucet running. As he wiped my arms and hands, he made me swear I'd never eat earth again.

I swore and Walter stroked my head. With his hand on my head, I couldn't tell if he was taller or if I had shrunk.

"Now brush your teeth," he said, leaving me in the bathroom on my own.

I looked in the mirror, smiled: my teeth were mud-stained. I thought of Papá and his smokes, the scent and darkness of his mouth, of how they wanted to forget him and how that was probably for the best. I held my brush under the stream of water, squeezed on some toothpaste, got everything wet, started brushing.

I walked back to the kitchen and tried one last time:

"Your brother's alive."

Tía turned around and looked furiously at me. She pulled a pack of smokes from her jean pocket.

"Filthy brat. I catch you eating dirt again and I'll burn your tongue with a lighter."

For a while, I was so scared I couldn't bring myself to even step on the earth, and avoided going outside without shoes on. Whenever I felt like eating dirt, I'd scarf down piping hot food, the second Tía took it off the stove. I wouldn't wait. I'd stuff my mouth and feel it blister. Then, tongue scorched, I'd down one glass after another of water. Belly full, the urge to scarf earth went away. The next day, I could hardly eat, I could hardly talk.

In time, they stopped messing with us at school. No more earth in my backpack dirtying my notebooks followed by muffled sniggers. No more alfajor wrappers—sweets I wanted but couldn't buy—filled with dirt sitting on my chair. Just the odd look, and a lot of silence.

And, without the earth, everything was perfect.

Until Señorita Ana stopped coming to school.

They looked for her, they said, behind the reedbed.

Not me.

I stared at the corner of the school courtyard where she'd stood watching Walter and the other kids play soccer. She didn't want any of the brats climbing the tree in the back, in case they fell.

I waited.

Once the police stopped looking for her among the weeds and little houses, or by the arroyo, I looked for her on the edge of the courtyard, in the dirt where her lovely boots had once stood to watch us play.

The urge had passed; I didn't know if I'd see anything. Still, I ran my hands through the earth and thought of how Señorita Ana wasn't turning up. I didn't want to lose her. I thought of Señorita Ana, alive. Of Señorita Ana, laughing. Then I made a fist and tried to make some part of her find its way into my palm, my mouth.

Even though everybody said those white smocks were pretty, I always thought they were crap. They got dirty. Mine had earth all over the cuffs. The front and neckline were fouled up.

On my way home, I thought of Tía smoking and of her lighters. When I got there, I pulled off my smock, balled it up, and hid it among the plants. I told Tía I'd left it at school, that I'd been made to take it off in gym class.

"I'm getting sick of this," she said. "I look after you all 'cause your old lady died and my brother up and left, but you don't listen."

She carried on cooking in the kitchen. I couldn't tell if she was talking to me or to herself:

"Don't like kids, never had any of my own."

I walked to the table hoping she'd snap out of it, and no longer heard her. A little later, Walter came and sat next to me. When Walter was tired, he always spread his legs real wide.

Tía carried a pot in from the kitchen.

"Go grab the plates," she told Walter. "And you, bring three glasses and three forks."

Just as we were getting up, Tía laid her hand on my wrist and said:

"Brush me off one more time, and it's over. Got it?"

"You, drawing by the window, get up," said the hall monitor sent to fetch me the next day. I didn't breathe a word. I knew I was in for it. I grabbed my drawing with both hands and walked behind him to the principal's office. Everybody stared.

Tía was there. She didn't have a clue what was going on. She'd come in to complain about my missing smock.

"What's wrong?" I asked. "What're you looking at me like that for?"

That was the last time I remember her looking, 'cause as soon as they saw the drawing, she and the principal forgot all about me.

It was Señorita Ana, her face just the way I remembered it, except not how she looked at school. I'd drawn her as the earth had shown me: naked, her legs spread-eagle and kind of bent, so that she looked smaller, like a frog. Her hands were behind her, tied to the posts of an open warehouse with the words "PANDA JUNKYARD" painted on it.

"What the fuck were you thinking, eating earth in front of the whole school?" my tía asked me at home, before slapping me.

When they found Señorita Ana's body on Panda Junkyard land the next day, Tía left. Neither Walter nor I ever heard from her again.

I wasn't going to school.

It was just Walter, his buddies, who came and went, and me.

I spent half the day slumped between my bed and the sofa by the door. My brother had got a job at a body shop. Sometimes, when he left for work, I would be slouched on the sofa, and when he came back, I'd still be there, staring at my toes.

Thinking: Why me, earth?

Walter never said a word. At noon, he would bring something for us to eat then head back to the shop. He was worried 'cause I'd quit school, but worry was all he could do. Half the kids in our barrio were dropouts. Except I wasn't working, and I wasn't knocked up either. All I did was laze about and sweep the house a little like I was trying to keep something from, I don't know, intruding.

Walter's friends were the only people who ever came by.

After five months of work, my brother bought himself a Play-Station and every weekend was a carnival: friends, PlayStation, pizza. We had a TV, but our cable had been cut and we never hooked it up again, so it was only good for gaming.

The boys were interested in one thing: soccer. When there was a game on, they went to Hernán's and I was left on my own. Hernán was the only friend of my brother's who paid any attention to me. He started bringing me music, knockoff CDs that we played on the console. I said "hey" and "thank you" and not much else, and he, a couple of times, came out with: "you're never alone when you've got music."

I had trouble sleeping. I nodded off a bunch of times a day and then, at night, it was all: eyes wide open, twisting, turning, pondering.

I started taking beers from the fridge, cracking them open and drinking them. I had kept my old man's bottle opener—the only thing of his I had left—and was always carrying it around in some pocket. Beer was like a blanket hug that covered me from top to bottom, my head most of all.

I only ever saw my old man in dreams. After waking up and not getting back to sleep, I'd play the music Hernán had left me until the very end. I had a stack of twelve CDs. Half of them read "compilation" and had a picture on the cover of some chick in a thong. Those ones, I stared at. The others, I popped into the PlayStation. I liked them better. When the beer ran out, the music kept on playing, and I drifted off.

Walter didn't notice 'cause I never drank with him and his friends. But one day he found me asleep with two empty bottles lying on their sides at the foot of the sofa. He wasn't mad.

"I've been leaving you on your own," he said, sitting down next to me.

My head hurt like next-level hell.

When he woke me up, I still felt queasy and weighed each step between me and the bathroom against the need to puke, which throttled my stomach.

We sat there, chatting a while. He told me what he'd been up to that night and I felt like I had nothing to share. But I liked that Walter was there with me.

I didn't have family, I had Walter.

We sat like that on the sofa for a couple of hours, till we heard clapping. Somebody was calling us from behind the property gate. We couldn't see much, so we both went out. It'd been a long time since I'd walked outside with no shoes on. I felt the dew and the chilly earth on my feet, and it did me more good than splashing my face with water a thousand times.

When we got near her, the woman who'd clapped her hands spoke:

"I've come to ask a favor."

My brother and I made eye contact and my head split again, as though her voice were another swig of booze. Neither of us moved and the woman didn't look like she wanted to leave. She was dressed in elegant clothes.

"Open up," I told Walter, and my brother undid the lock.

"What sort of favor?" I asked the woman when she came through.

"Help. I need your help."

We went inside. The house was a dump, dingy like an animal's lair. But the woman seemed to have eyes only for me. She sat down without a word. She waited, as though being there, beside us, were an important part of what she had come to do.

When my brother went to the kitchen to put the kettle on for mate, she asked:

"Do you have vision?"

She said it quietly, like a secret.

"No."

"Don't lie to me. Do you have vision?!"

Thick bitch, I thought. Though I didn't like it, her question forced me to take a hard look at myself. I'd never thought of what I did as vision. Vision was a strange thing, like believing I could guess the winning bet. Which had nothing to do with closing your eyes and being faced with a naked body on the earth.

"No. I used to, but not anymore."

"Did you try just now?"

Walter had come back, so I didn't answer. How did she know about us? The woman wouldn't shut up, though. She said she needed our help, that she'd heard there was someone here, in this house, who could see, that she had money and was willing to shell out a tidy sum.

"We don't need your money," I said.

"But I need you."

Hernán walked in, shoving the door open. We hadn't put the lock back on the gate and he'd let himself through. He'd brought a new CD. I was scared he might hear the woman say the thing about sight.

I was frozen in place. Walter sent her packing, as though he felt the same way.

Before she left, the woman knelt down, righted the two bottles by the sofa, and said:

"You drink this junk for kicks. Won't you eat earth 'cause somebody needs it?"

I felt like beating the shit out of her but stayed right where I was. I couldn't even look at Hernán. As I watched the woman walk across the yard, I took a deep breath and slowly let it all out, till I was empty. Only when Walter locked the gate did I breathe.

Hernán had put a CD in the PlayStation. The music was getting started.

I bet she waited for Walter to leave. Alone, lips sealed. Not moving the slightest. A woman looking for her son can turn invisible, like a cat stalking a pigeon.

I got it, she was looking for somebody.

I'd started noticing a special trait in people who were looking for someone, a mark near the eyes, the mouth, a mixture of pain, anger, strength, and expectation made flesh. A thing broken, possessed by the person who wasn't coming back.

I opened the door and let the woman in. She sat opposite me. She set a can down on the table and stared. Didn't even blink. What was it? Money? Chocolate? Fancy folk can do that, I thought, stuff a bunch of chocolate and cash in a can and set it right in front of you. So you'll say yes, even if you don't want to.

I didn't like her.

She started talking. For her husband, she said, it was always nothing: sometimes kids fall behind, sometimes kids disappear. It had been like that in the past, when Ian was two years old and still couldn't walk, and it was like that now, when he was sixteen and hadn't come home.

I didn't want to listen, not for all the chocolate in the world. But she went on: that his absence was killing her, that her body hurt more now than when she'd given birth to him.

"Ian," she said. "My son. He never hurt a soul, you know. He couldn't."

Scared she'd never shut up, I cut in.

"What's in the can?"

"Earth."

I didn't want to, but the woman opened the can and left it there, and the memory of earth turned to water in my mouth. Dark earth shone inside and some part of me responded without words.

I didn't want to, but my body did. I touched the dirt like it meant everything. I pulled it toward me without lifting it from the table.

"Turn around," I said. "You can't watch."

She didn't much like that. She took her time, mulled it over, then got up and turned her chair to face the other way. She didn't try to steal a look.

I grabbed some earth from the can and bit by bit stuffed it in my mouth.

The house grew dark, like it'd been covered in a black sheet. I had the urge to switch on the light. To keep the night, which the earth had unfurled around us, from swallowing us up. Everything was so dark, so like a deep well untouched by the sun, no good could come of it. When I was about to stop, to quit out of fear and open my eyes, the darkness retreated, as if somebody had lit some candles, one by one. My eyes got used to seeing again.

Though I couldn't make out much, I heard everything clearly. Her voice. The woman's. She said, screamed: *Ian*. And after yelling his name over and over, there, in the brightest spot, in the heart of the light, a little boy around eight years old emerged.

He wasn't a clever pup but a strange, lost-looking boy. The light that shone from his body was weak, sickly, sad. The woman kept saying "Ian, Ian" without waiting for an answer.

She gripped him hard by the hand and started tugging at him. I tried to make out the boy but couldn't. A man appeared beside the woman and spoke to her:

"Did you find him?"

"Yeah. Can't leave the kid alone, not even to pee."

"Where was he?"

"Behind the birthday party. On his own."

"Who took him there?"

"I did, thought he could wait five minutes."

Like a secret, a secret the man didn't want to know, they fell quiet. They were looking at him. Then the man asked:

"Why'd you leave him on his own?"

"'Cause I can't right take him to the bathroom with me, can I? He's eleven."

"Means nothing, though. His age means nothing," the man said and they both went quiet again, as though the sad light that radiated from Ian were weakening their bodies, too.

The man got mad again and recovered some of his strength.

"Stop making excuses. Don't you care about him?"

The boy stood between them. Then he began to shuffle to the side. Like he wasn't even listening. He looked up, ahead of him. I tried to make out what he saw but found nothing.

They spoke as if the little boy wasn't there. I tried to get a better look, but he slipped away from me. The voices grew quieter and quieter. I got tired of trying to listen to what they said, of trying to see what the earth chose not to show me.

I opened my eyes.

The house was darker than the night that swaddled the lost boy.

"It's no use," I told the woman. "I can barely see him. Only you, doña. Arguing with a man who keeps asking why you left Ian alone."

The woman grew even sadder. All of a sudden, she bounced back and said:

"His dad."

"I can see the two of you, doña. But the kid keeps slipping away."

The woman dropped her head and cried in silence. She opened her purse. To look for something to dry her eyes with, I thought, except she pulled out a wad of money and a stack of photographs instead. She placed the pictures on the notes—there were so many of them—and pushed them toward me. It was the little snot. I thumbed through the first few photos. In them, he was older and wore the same lost expression.

"That's not how it works."

"Okay," she said, looking up. "So how do we make it work?"

Hernán laughed on his moped.

"It's not that far," he said. "How come you've never been?"

I said nothing. I didn't even go to the grocery store anymore.

"We're close, already on Route 8."

That much I knew. I also knew about the market, which had opened a couple of years ago. But no, I'd never been.

"What should we hit: Mega or Fericrazy?"

I laughed.

"What do I know. Whichever you're most into."

"Mega," read a billboard over the entrance to the road, and I could make out a parking lot thronged with mopeds, people, and cars. The road was in fucking bad shape. We kept having to dodge water, mud, trash.

"Let's go to that one," I said, pointing to the spot where buses stopped to let out smiling families.

Hernán parked the bike as close to the entrance as he could. He tried to say something, but it was so noisy I couldn't hear him.

"Inside," I mouthed, and we started walking.

A massive warehouse. Concrete floor. No real plants, just gross plastic ones. I'd never felt so far from the earth and I didn't like it one bit.

I opened my backpack and for a split-second showed it to Hernán, like it was a game. He went real wide-eyed, and asked:

"Where'd you get a hold of so much cash?"

"I got it and that's that. What do you care?" I said with a smile.

"You aren't going around sticking people up, are you?"

We both cracked up.

"We're gonna make it rain," I said, brandishing a couple of five-hundred-peso notes, and shaking them in the air. Hernán laughed.

"For sure," he said, winking.

We strolled. There were four rows of stands, one next to the other. The passages between were crammed full of people. Everybody looked happy. On a corner, people hawked sweets as though it was a public square: candied almonds, popcorn, chocolate peanuts. I took some cotton candy and tried to pay with a five-hundred-peso bill. "I haven't got any change," the woman serving me said. Hernán pulled out twenty pesos and handed it to her. I put mine away.

"Girl, you're gonna cost me steep," he said and took my hand.

It felt weird but good.

He took me to a beer counter where a guy was emptying bottles into disposable cups. Each cup held a liter for the hands awaiting them. "Two," I ordered and paid. I pocketed the change and we walked on. Cotton candy in one hand and a liter of beer in the other. We paused in front of an enormous booth. Strings of movies in plastic sleeves that hung in rows on the front and sides. Boxes filled with CDs and DVDs and a bunch of folks flipping through them. The movies were sorted by category: Domestic, New Release, Comedy, XXX, Horror.

"These are the ones I'm always bringing you," Hernán said, gesturing toward two boxes. He took a real long sip from his disposable cup. The first box was for "compilations" and there was a chick in a red thong and a Santa Claus hat. The other just said "Latinos." I browsed that one. I turned each sleeve over and read the song titles. I set three aside. Hernán asked to see them so he could check out the list of songs, too. We glanced at one another and laughed.

"Your mouth's full of pink goo," he said, and I felt the beer go to my head. I sucked on two of my fingers so he wouldn't have the chance to complain about my sticky hands too.

"Let's see," he said, and came up to me. He gave me a long kiss, a sugary mix of lips, beer, and his soft tongue, which I loved. I wanted more, but Hernán pulled away.

"Best check out the CDs instead. Your brother's gonna kill me."

We laughed. Why should Walter give a shit?

In the end, we picked out five CDs and Hernán threw in a horror flick. He said we could watch it later on the PlayStation if there was nobody around. I said maybe we should eat something first. We paid and they handed us a bag, which I shoved in my backpack, and made our way toward the stands in the back. Hernán drank his whole beer. I still had half left, so I shared it with him.

We ordered two cheeseburgers and fries. We didn't wait long. We ate with our hands at a table for two. They didn't sell beer there, only pop, so we didn't order anything to drink. We made do with what was left in my cup.

"These fries are mad good," Hernán said a couple seconds after he'd finished chewing. "Let's head back to yours?"

I nodded yes. Where else would we go? But then I thought of my brother. I hadn't even told him I was going out with Hernán.

"Let's get Walter a present first," I said, and he agreed right away.

I don't know if the scent of patties was from our burgers or if the warehouse was thick with smoke. The massive Mega warehouse was windowless and the exit was through the entrance. The smoke from the food skidded against our bodies and against the clothes draped on the coat hangers in the booths. Bringing something for Walter also meant bringing him a little bit of all this. And I liked that.

Where'd you get the money?" my brother asked, unable to stifle a huge smile.

"You like it, though?"

He held up the jacket and stared at it like the thing was a ghost. I thought of Hernán trying it on for size, which made me giggle. There'd be no movie that night. Some other time.

"I've been working. Took on a gig." My brother kept mum, so I carried on. "I'm helping that woman from the other day. She's paid me."

For a second, I thought Walter hadn't heard me: he wasn't talking or moving or even glancing my way. He wasn't getting mad either. Nothing. Then, he looked up at me.

"You sure, lil sis? If you're doing it for the money, don't."

"It'll all be all right," I said without thinking. "I'm sure of it."

My brother came up to me and kissed me on the cheek. Then he said the jacket was awesome and asked me where I got it. I laughed.

"It's a surprise, Walter."

He took it to his room, saying he'd wear it some other time. It was special so he was gonna put it away for now.

The same can on the table and the woman, looking stern and saying she'd brought the right earth this time.

"How am I supposed to know?" I didn't want to eat dirt every day.

I walked around. Bided my time. Went to the kitchen and put the kettle on even though I knew I wouldn't be drinking mate till later. That day, I wanted to be able to say no.

"Mate?"

The woman shook her head. Annoyed, I went to the kitchen and turned off the burner.

I came back in. Averted my eyes.

"I've got a stomachache."

"I didn't come yesterday," the woman said, and I felt kind of sorry for her.

"News on Ian?"

"The cops have stopped looking for him."

I studied her, then. She had these awful bags under her eyes; her neck and jowls were flabby and starting to wrinkle. But she had strong arms. She sat firm and upright as she waited for me to grab the can. I knew the woman wouldn't let up till I found him. She was starting to grow on me.

Walter came out of his room, spotted her sitting there, and stalked off in silence. He didn't even say hello. Him leaving like that rubbed me the wrong way.

Sometimes I thought that if my brother never came back, I could have eaten all the dirt in the house—I could've broken it, made it quake.

"Hand it over," I said and she nudged the tin toward me.

Hope she's done it right, I thought to myself, but said nothing. I was no chump.

I ate some of the woman's earth but instead of thinking about the little snot, I thought of Hernán's kiss, of the cotton candy and beer from the day before.

I closed my eyes and saw her.

It was like returning to a night long ago. A night that had been wearing out and had ceased to exist and that I could only see from there, from that moment, in my head.

Ian looked worn-out, too. Like he was high. The man pushed him. He didn't cry. He wore his usual expression, except frightened. The man had on green overalls and stared at Ian. I recognized him. I didn't like him one bit. He stared at the little snot like he was sizing him up. Ian could barely stand. His eyes drooped and his head flopped side to side. He shook himself, trying to pry his eyes open again and stand up straight. It was like the air had turned strange.

Ian fell. His body was on the floor now. The man sat beside the boy, but with his back to him; Ian, who'd smacked his head on the ground, bled.

The man was Ian's father. His eyes had been glued on his son, but now that the boy's body was spent, on the ground, the man was pretending he wasn't there. He pulled a lighter from his overall pocket and began to smoke. He looked down at the cigarette and then ahead of him, past the smoke, somewhere I couldn't see. He smoked for a while, calm.

Then, he got up.

He walked toward a car. Try as I might I couldn't make out the license plate. He opened the back door and grabbed a couple of black trash bags. He rooted around for something else, didn't find it, and gave up. He went back to Ian and lifted him. He walked away, the boy's body and the trash bags in his arms, and he lumbered through some real tall weeds. I tried to follow but couldn't. They were out of my sightline and I had trouble moving. No matter how hard I tried, I couldn't go forward. Little by little, I went stiff. Like a statue. I was trapped in that bullshit. I gazed down, hunting for earth, but found only trash engulfing my shoes. I gazed ahead and tried to find the man stealing his boy's body. But the trash mushroomed into mountains. The stench penetrated my nose, as though it were a swarm of furious wasps beating their way out of my head, hurting me.

I opened my eyes. The stench still stung. It reminded me of the smell of dead dogs on the roadside.

I looked at the woman, strong arms clasping her purse.

She waited for me to speak. I waited for the stench to leave me alone.

I didn't know whether she'd like what I had to say.

I was washing my face when Hernán came by. I was the sort who never cried. I shoved my hands back under the cold water. My eyes stung and my hands burned, but worst of all was Ian's dirt inside my body. Still clamoring to speak.

Hernán put on some music, *Cri cri minal* the song went, over and over, and I don't know why that made me want to cry too. I patted myself dry with a towel and glanced in the mirror. I never used to cry. I tried to keep my eyes open so as not to see what the earth wanted to show me. My eyes kept tearing. I thought of the woman and hoped she'd never come back. She had asked me to see but hadn't been able to stomach what I saw.

Tú me robaste el corazón como un criminal, the song went. You stole my heart like a criminal. I didn't want to listen. The earth churned in my stomach. That curly-haired boy was rooted in my belly like a son in his mama's heart.

I needed him out. I turned on the faucet as far as it would go, so the sound of running water would carry him away.

I kneeled at the toilet and shoved two fingers down my throat till I gagged. Farther. It hurt. I threw up.

I forgot because I could. I'd never be a mother. I didn't want to be a mother.

I went back to the faucet, eyes down. I put my hands, then my arms under the stream of water. I took them out, then stuck my face under, and my smarting eyes, which I was finally able to close. The water was healing. I relaxed. I pulled my head out from under the water, turned off the faucet, groped around for a towel, and slowly, as if stroking a burned body, dried myself off. I walked out.

Hernán asked me what was wrong, like he'd seen a ghost.

"Nothing," I said. "Slept like shit."

He was quiet. I don't think he believed me, but he didn't say anything else.

Cri cri minal had ended, and I decided I didn't want to listen to music. I felt bad for Hernán, but I just couldn't. I went to the PlayStation and switched it off.

"I can leave if you want," he said with wide eyes.

I bit my lip. I browsed the stack my brother kept by the Play-Station, grabbed a sleeve, picked it up.

"Why don't you teach me how to game instead?"

Round 1 Fight flashed onscreen, and I started.

Hernán insisted I couldn't fight if I kept laughing, and since I wanted to win I tried not to laugh. At first, I pressed the buttons as fast as I could. But instead of taking cover, my character kept leaping back, and Hernán cracked up.

"Check out the moves list," he said.

Huh.

"What moves list?"

"Finish this round and I'll show you."

I was up against Sheeva. Her body was dark, and she had six brawny arms to fuck me up with. Her bra, like every female character in *Mortal Kombat*, showed her tits. I'd gone for Sub-Zero, a dude. I liked not needing to worry about having a huge rack, even in a videogame. I'm a twig.

"Hand it over," Hernán said once I beat Sheeva. "Check this out."

He pressed a button and a list of special moves popped up on the screen. Forward—Forward—Punch. Forward—Forward—Kick. That sort of thing. And all the way at the bottom, fatalities.

I returned to combat. This time, against Raiden. I got in a few kicks and he immediately poured down on me. I tried out a few special moves. I felt happy for the five seconds it took Sub-Zero's hands to fill with ice before he hurled that deadly chill at his opponent, freezing him stiff. Then, I hit Raiden from up close and his body shot backward and smashed on the ground.

Raiden sprung up to retaliate and I pressed *start*.

"It doesn't count if you pause the game all the time," Hernán said. I reminded him he had insisted I use the moves list.

"I haven't figured even half of it out yet," I retorted, pressing *start* again and pausing the game.

"You're such a cheat," he said, and we laughed.

"Last time, I'm ready now," I promised, even though it was a lie.

"I can see that," said Hernán and he laughed. "You're so bent on winning, you're not learning how to play."

I feigned anger so as not to admit he was right. But I kept going back to the list of moves. I practiced one on the joystick and felt like I was finally getting it. I was ready, I pressed *start*. I went up to Raiden and tried the combo. This time, it worked. The slugging he took drained his health and the words *FINISH HIM!* flashed onscreen. Raiden wobbled centerstage and I ended him.

For a time after Mamá died, I was convinced Tía and Walter would die too. I didn't really care about Tía but it fucked me up to picture my brother dead. I would hide away and cry for hours. Then, I started to think of how I could die too, and hard as I might try I couldn't picture it. Instead, I imagined a dog dragging one of its legs. The dog got sicker and sicker from a tumor in her spine, and I imagined her limping with her leg towed behind her, down the highway, around the neighborhood, and through our front door, her leg progressively mangled by the ground. The tumor grew, like tits on a girl. Thinner and thinner, the dog lost both her appetite and the desire to move. I pictured her wasting away against the property gate and, in her flesh, glimpsed my own death.

Raiden was dead and I was jumping around like a nutso. Hernán too. We hugged. Just as he was about to kiss me on the lips, Walter walked in.

'd been at the PlayStation for two weeks. At first, I had a hard time choosing between music and games. Then, I figured it out: games at night and music when I went to bed.

It was Sunday and Walter didn't have work. I was happy 'cause it was the first time he was letting me play with everyone. I ran through the moves in my head. I had a pretty good grasp on the ones for Sub-Zero, Sonya, and Raiden. The others, hardly at all.

Whenever somebody came through, they would start at the fridge, where they left a couple of beers. Everybody did the same. Then, they headed into the room for a spot. There wasn't space for another soul. There were kids on the bed, the floor, on my brother's bench, kids standing around clutching beers—the room was slammed.

"Sit your ass on my pillow and that's the last thing you'll do," Walter said.

Hernán hadn't arrived yet. Though at first I pretended not to mind, I really wanted him to show already. Two weeks of practicing together and today was the day he decided to skip out?

But there he was. He said hi to everybody and held something up for us to see.

"It was at the entrance," he said. "It's heavy as fuck."

"It's probably the Iglesia Universal paper," my brother said from the floor where he sat by the door.

Hernán headed to the bed. He wound his way through several people to get to me.

"Look," he said, handing it over.

Everybody stared at me, and I, surrounded by all those boys, took the package and pretended it was nothing.

"What's up?" Walter asked.

I didn't answer. I got off the bed and tiptoed through the legs of the folks on the floor on my way out the door. Hernán took my seat. There were people in every room, so I headed to the bathroom. My brother slipped in behind me, then looked at me. I lifted the package so he could see how fat it was. Walter told me to open it. He shut the door, pressing his weight against it to stop people coming in.

I held the package. I could tell they had weighted the bottom, carefully fastening the package so it wouldn't come open. As I cut the thread with my teeth, I couldn't help catching my reflection in the mirror, biting and baring my teeth. I didn't like it at all. I sealed my lips. Tried to fix my hair, to look more like myself. I tugged at the thread and eyed my reflection again.

I opened the envelope. Inside was a newspaper. I scanned the pages till I came across one with the words "thank you" scrawled in red marker pen and, circled in the same color, a news article: "Runaway Veterinarian Sole Suspect in Murder of Special Needs Teen." It was the man I'd seen. Except he wasn't wearing his green coveralls. He looked much younger in the paper, like the photo was taken before he had become Ian's father.

Inside the newspaper was a load of cash. I didn't want to count it, so my brother took it from me.

I stared at the man's photo. I knew they'd probably published his name in the paper, but I didn't want to read it. I looked at the photo from up close, searched for something in his eyes, but they were only that: two eyes that expressed nothing. Would anyone remember what he had been like before he became a father? I had only seen him after.

Walter slowly counted the money. When he finished, he said:

"Damn . . . It's a shitload. Enough for a PlayStation 4." Neither of us laughed.

In the paper was also a black-and-white photo of Ian. He wasn't smiling either, his eyes angled upward. If I could've been beside him and followed his gaze, I thought, I would most likely have found that he was staring at nothing, at least nothing I could see. Beneath the photo: "His body was discovered in . . ." but I didn't want to read on.

I closed the paper and handed it to Walter.

A few days later, we lost our phone line.

We didn't miss it. Sometimes I thought there was nothing we missed anymore, that we could adapt to anything so long as we, my brother and me, were together.

We didn't miss the phone 'cause we hardly ever called anybody and hardly anybody ever called us. Our friends just dropped in; the rest steered clear. The week after we got the package, the phone rang a lot. Whenever one of us answered, a voice said:

"You're gonna scream, bitch."

My brother got sick of it and cut the line with a knife. Ta-da, no more phone.

For the first few days, my brother skipped work and stayed with me.

Which was even worse.

Walter was leery of cell phones, the front door, the cars that rolled past, even the handful of zombies that crept up our block after a night out. Everything was on lockdown. Us and the house, in the dark all day long.

I wanted Hernán to come by. Whenever he did, Walter stood his ground and didn't let us get a word in without him listening. So Hernán would just eat and drink a bunch of crap and come up with an excuse to leave.

One afternoon, you could slice the air with a knife. I opened the door and sat on the floor without venturing out. Walter said nothing.

As a storm brewed outside, I started to cry. My brother sat beside me. I couldn't remember the last time we'd watched the rain together, if that was something we ever did. I looked up at the sky, then at the droplets battering our land. It was like the rain swept everything away.

The next day was a Friday and the night was thick with kids.

Hernán came through early. He was twitchy. I don't think he could put up with my brother anymore either, which was painful to watch. I wanted them to stay friends.

As the boys trickled in, my brother went back to his usual self. And for a few hours, the rest of the world melted away.

We played like we used to when we were little kids, unworried, wanting only to win.

Then, around one, a boy came through. Said there was a car parked by the gate. I thought Walter would tell us to stay put, indoors, locked up, but he and Hernán wanted to check it out right away, like they'd agreed on it beforehand. The rest of us abandoned the PlayStation, walked out of the room, followed them to the door. Not two minutes passed before we heard screaming. We couldn't see anything, so we all stepped outside.

"No, not you," my brother yelled as soon as he saw me. "Back inside."

Till that moment I'd had eyes only for him and Hernán. Then I turned my head and glimpsed the car. That's when I saw the guy. It was dark out and he wasn't in green coveralls, but it was him. His eyes. Though his son couldn't follow or focus his eyes on anything for more than thirty seconds, the father's eyes could pierce bodies. Fear enveloped me and left me frozen in the front yard of my house. I tried to go inside but couldn't move.

How was I seeing him? I thought of the vision and wondered if I'd seen him with the same eyes that looked at him now or with some other part of my body.

Still staring, he turned on the engine and pulled out a gun. There was no time. All I knew was I didn't want to watch him kill me. I turned around and heard gunshots, the revving car, and my breath, my furious heart, my body springing to life.

One of the bullets struck the water tank and water rained from the roof. My brother touched me. It was dark and we could barely see. I had the urge to hug him. Slowly, as if thawing out, we began to move.

I turned to face the street. The car was gone but I still wanted to have a look.

I don't know if he was a bad shot or if he hadn't wanted to kill us. Either way, he missed.

Walter was saying it's all right, the guy's gone, that he could remember the car and would go talk to the cops. He told me to stay inside, to play a game or listen to some music, that he'd take care of everything. Unlike my brother, Hernán was quiet and distant.

Walter led me inside by the arm. We saw a huge bullet hole over the doorway. Nobody breathed a word.

As the sun rose, I drifted off. I didn't hear my brother leave, but we'd agreed he should file a report with the cuffs. Even if we didn't like it one fucking bit.

I slept like in a coma and woke up late feeling like I'd been hit by a train. There was no water and my brother was asking his buddies to go to the junkyard with him for a new tank. They all said yeah, they'd help him buy it, bring it home, it was no bother. But when Walter asked them to keep me company—he didn't want to leave me alone—they all went quiet. So my brother took a wad of cash out of his pocket and handed it to them, and they said they'd handle it, that's what friends were for, they'd hit the junkyard and be back in no time. They'd help him change the tank too.

Once they had left, Walter looked at me and said:

"We're on our own again, lil sis. Just the two of us. Can't blame them."

I was quiet. I didn't expect anything from anyone either.

If it wasn't their fault, whose was it? My body's? I couldn't change what my body saw.

I went to the bathroom and peed. Then I scrubbed my face, trying not to check my reflection in the mirror.

When I came out, it was just Walter and me. He put the kettle on. Tried to get us to buck up. We didn't talk about it, but I knew he was right. We were alone because of what I saw.

Hernán had left in the morning. He didn't even take his joystick. No kiss, no *chau*, nothing. As I smoked and stared out at the street, I knew I couldn't expect his music to come back through that door.

Part Two

The sun dried everything that yesterday's rain had turned to puddle and mud, wiping away the footprints of those who were gone: Mamá, our old man, Tía, Hernán, all of them leaving single file like those ants that, no matter how much you set them on fire, keep building their homes underground, where there's no green nor sunshine and where Florensia's flesh was turning to bone.

The grass was overrun with weeds. The bay laurel was out of control and grew wherever it pleased. A thousand seedlings that, struck by the sun, shot up and bent the wire around our land like cardboard.

Some plant or other had gotten stuck to the corrugated iron wall and rotted into a stain on the side of the house. Above, passionflower, like in the properties around the abandoned line. Once it blossomed, the flower buzzed with bees hypnotized by the cross at its center, by its dampness and gummy filaments.

If my hair keeps growing, I thought, *I can become a wild and strong-legged plant too, daughter of the bay laurel.*

No one had yanked me out in time; there I was now, on the stoop, hugging my legs.

Someone tossed a piece of paper over the property fence and I followed it with my eyes. They didn't care to clap or call out, too scared to even say my name. The wind whipped the paper across the tall grass. "GOD LOVES YOU," it read and I wished the wind would take it away from there, past the wire fence, which was as far as I went barefoot. There were no voices anymore to say: "Your feet are trailing muck."

"You've got mud in your teeth and fingers," said the mother of my classmate, Florencia, when she decided to stop letting her hang out with me.

Others didn't have the guts to come through the gate and instead would leave their loved one's earth in bottles. They'd leave a card, too, and slung around the bottleneck, a name. I took the bottles and arranged them in the plants. The sun glinted off them. Whenever it rained too heavily, the water crept inside and overflowed, mixing their earth with mine.

Every bottle was a morsel of earth that could speak.

Marta, Florensia's mother, did come past the gate. It'd been years since I'd seen her. She barged in like she owned the place. She wanted to pay for "the appointment," she said.

"No, Marta. I can't take your money."

As we stepped into my house, I didn't mention to Marta—who

52

thought she was all that 'cause she and Florensia went to church on Sundays, her girl blonde and promising as a red paper wasp—that I had missed her daughter after she stopped letting her come over.

The thing is, I saw Marta's eyes. Pure dark circles from crying.

We went in so that I could sit down and she could park her fat ass on the tiny sofa of my "suite," and so that I could eat the earth she had brought with her out of the palm of her hand and so that she could ask, always nosing around, always in a rush:

"What do you see? What do you see?"

A car drove past blaring *corazón de seda, que no lo tiene cualquiera* and I thought of Florensia's clothes, which weren't as tattered as her skin, and of Florensia, down there, like the roots of our land's plants and the stubborn ants marching down their tunnels.

Marta wouldn't shut up. She was starting to get on my nerves. She thought she was better than everybody 'cause the only blonde head in the barrio belonged to her Florensia and—in church, made of plaster—to baby Jesus.

"What do you see? What do you see?"

I had to gather strength to open my eyes and say:

"Settle down, Marta. I see a lot of light."

I had never cried with eyes shut. I saw Florensia, maggot-ridden like a sickly heart, her hair a spiderweb peeling off her skull.

"Settle down, Marta, seeing hurts my eyes. She's fine. Her hair looks like it's catching the sun."

Marta breathed again, so deeply her chest looked bigger than her ass.

"Open your eyes then, nena. Why are you crying?" she said as she gripped me with both hands. Though her hands were warm, I kept my eyes sealed. I wondered: *Is Florensia cold down there in the earth—so unlike swimming, so unlike being formed long ago in that woman's warm belly?*

Florensia's mother wouldn't let go. This time, the earth didn't make her shudder. She didn't even notice the muck under my nails.

"She'll come visit once she's back, I'm sure she will."

"Go easy, Marta. You won't have to look after her anymore. Florensia was always such a beautiful girl. God loves her."

I walked Marta to the gate in my bare feet and stood around barefoot killing time, glancing down at the bottles stashed in the plants. Some had been there a while and were slowly becoming buried, rooted, their letters and names and phone numbers soiled by water and by time, which blotted out everything but the pain of the person who'd brought them there and the need—all gone but one—to know where they were.

I didn't know about the house. But the earth, underneath everything, was mine.

That night, I dreamed of Señorita Ana. I don't know if it was the first time or if I'd forgotten other dreams. But I never forgot her.

Though years had passed and I had shot up, Señorita Ana looked way taller than me that night, just as she'd always been. She asked me from up high about the other girls in my grade. I told her I'd bumped into so-and-so in the grocery store or shared a story I'd heard from Walter; I didn't see them anymore myself. We ate toasted sunflower seeds and Señorita Ana asked me about each of them, one by one, except for Florensia. She knew. I told her I'd seen Candela and that she was knocked up, that Sofi had moved in around the corner with a guy who drove about on a moped for work.

"My brother said they're expecting," I said, and Señorita Ana fell into a deep silence.

She passed me some more seeds and I tossed them in my mouth, spitting out the shells. She wasn't impressed. She hadn't been impressed before, either: she was always saying we made a big old mess of those sunflower seeds.

"I would've like to," Señorita Ana said then.

"See 'em?" I asked.

She stared into the distance. Filled her lungs with air and then let out:

"I would've liked to get pregnant, too. Have a baby girl. Like all of you."

She looked at me and I avoided her eyes.

"Not me, hell no. Girls go missing," I said, quickly stuffing my mouth with seeds.

Señorita Ana stared at me. Like the bag of sunflower seeds, I thought, something in her was running out too.

After that, we stopped talking.

I woke up thirsty for beer.

The joke was straightforward, but not even those I got.

Walter said:

"I've got twenty lice on me. Gonna have to wash my hair with kerosene."

And I'd sit there wondering how my brother knew there were twenty bugs in his hair.

Then, he and his friends would laugh and say they had twenty beers, and I'd count the ones they brought in. Sometimes five, ten, or around fifteen, but never twenty. At some point I realized he wasn't saying "twenty" but "plenty," though not even that made me laugh.

I was thinking about that joke when I opened the outer gate and saw that another bottle had been snuck onto our land. I carried a bag on my arm with some bread, two cans of beer, and the sausages Walter liked. I was hurrying home from the grocery store 'cause I wanted to cook up the sausages before he got back from the shop.

As I locked the gate, I thought of how I had zero interest in finding another bottle. Of how I couldn't leave it there in case the few neighbors who still didn't know about me saw it or started picturing—as I was right then—a hand slipping through the gate and the desperate face of the person who'd brought the bottle. Anyway, even if I did pick it up, I didn't want to eat earth that day, end of story. As far as I was concerned, there'd been "twenty" bottles for a while. So many I couldn't even count them, so many they got on my nerves.

If you boil the sausages too long, they burst and end up like bland, blown-up chorizos. We ate them anyway on hot dog buns doused in mayo, but neither of us enjoyed it. That's how my head felt that day: like meat ready to burst.

As I walked toward the bottle, I made an effort not to read the message and to persuade myself it was written in Chinese. I prayed it hadn't come with a photo. The bottle was blue, broad, filled halfway with dirt. Crouching, I touched it. The feel of the glass stung the palm of my hand. I picked it up with the same arm that held the bag slung near my elbow.

Sometimes I could feel the weight of every single bottle turning my house into something I'd always despised: a graveyard crawling with strangers, a container of earth that spoke of bodies I'd never laid eyes on. Meanwhile, Mamá was all alone in the place where folks claimed the dead were laid to rest. I never visited her. I don't know about Walter. There were times when I wanted to go but didn't. I hadn't been back since she was taken away from me as a little girl.

I walked to the house with the bottle. I stared at it, not knowing if I liked it or not, if I'd open it or not, if I'd charge the person who'd left it or just not call them. All I wanted was for it to be me and my brother eating sausages on the living room sofa, my only worry making sure they didn't overcook, and that Walter didn't get ketchup and mayo all over himself.

The house key was in my shorts pocket. I wouldn't bring the bottle into the house that day, or call anyone, or scarf earth. Anyway, nobody was watching. I rounded the house thinking, as usual, of how I needed to tend to the plants but would just end up eating something yummy with my hands instead. That way there'd be no plates to wash. Then, I'd bum around with Walter.

I knelt down among the plants, parted the massive leaves, and put the bottle next to the others for company. There were plenty of blue ones. No blue was the same and no earth tasted alike. No child, sibling, mother, or friend was missed like another. Side by side, they were like glimmering tombs. At first, I used to count them and arrange them tenderly, sometimes stroking one until it let me savor the earth inside it. That was how I usually felt. But right then, I despised them. They weighed on me more than ever. Altogether, they exhausted me. I felt the bottles piling up on me. The world must be much larger than I'd imagined for so many people to have disappeared in it.

I retraced my steps and entered the house. I put on music, went to the kitchen, and turned on the burner. I looked for the kettle and filled it with water, trying not to think of how the person inside that bottle might die at any moment. I shoved the sausages to the bottom of the pot, one by one, till they were buried in water. I left them on the burner.

Walter arrived a few minutes later.

We ate the hot dogs, practically slopped over with mayonnaise, our fingers smeared, cold beers in hands, just the way it should be. My brother was happy; it was contagious. I didn't ask why. We shot the breeze. Walter did nearly all the talking, sometimes with his mouth full, chomping like an oaf. I listened and laughed with him.

Later, he kissed me on the cheek and went back to the shop. He wouldn't be home till later that night.

When he closed the door, I let my body drop on the living room sofa, where the day after and the next one and in the twenty days that followed, I would attend to people and scarf their earth and ask whether this person or that was alive or breathing and for how long and why had their lungs stopped or who had taken them. For now, all I wanted to do was sleep.

He stood against the gate. He looked real sad for someone so young. His hair was tidy and his clothes perfect, like in a cigarette ad.

I'd heard someone knock and, not awake yet, had taken my time to go outside.

He wasn't knocking anymore. Either he'd gotten tired or given up. He was waiting.

Spying me, he peeled himself off the gate. I stared at him in silence and didn't say half a word.

He'd come to the door that morning, he said. He'd actually been coming for days but hadn't been able to get himself out of the car.

Then he fell quiet and I looked him over.

He'd waited, he said, because he was looking for someone.

I didn't know what to say. All I wanted was more sleep. I didn't even know if Walter was home or if he'd left for the shop.

"I need help," he said, as a woman passed us on the sidewalk.

Her shopping cart screeched to a stop and she looked at me: a woman from the barrio.

I opened the door, turned around, and when I felt him walk in after me, said:

"Shut the door."

I didn't want anyone seeing him, much less folk talking shit about me. I hadn't even brushed my hair. I must look like a zombie.

I wasn't scared of him. Sitting there on the living room sofa, he was the one who seemed scared. As though he'd slept badly, like me.

"I didn't get any sleep," I said. "What do you want?"

"I'm looking for somebody," he said again, his eyes turned down and fixed on his hand.

He looked around ten years older than Walter, but in a button-down shirt, shoes, expensive clothes.

In the sadness of his face, he was like my brother and me. Also, in the slow way he had of speaking, like he was struggling to get his words out.

"Who're you looking for?" I said suppressing a yawn, my eyes teary from sleepiness.

He was quiet. It was still morning but I was thirsty for beer and wanted to go back to sleep.

"What's the point? Her name won't mean anything to you," he said, looking me head-on.

"I don't usually see people at this hour, but if you give me five minutes I'll hear you out."

I opened the fridge. Practically empty. Cold leftovers of some chicken Walter had brought home the day before. I breathed audibly. Nuh-uh, I was in no shape to eat earth. I closed it and went for the kettle, filled it with water, turned on the burner. I prepped the mate while the water boiled. Would he drink mate? I didn't know 'cause I didn't care. If he told me his story now, I wouldn't sleep easy all day. How could I stop him?

The water was ready. I turned off the fire, brought out the kettle and the mate, and set them in front of the sofa. He still looked like a weary man to me, a man worn out ahead of time.

"Do you drink mate?"

"Of course."

I stirred the leaves just a tad with the bombilla, then poured a stream of hot water into the hole in the middle. I handed him the mate and he drank it. Done, he held the empty mate in his hand and started to tell his story. He said his aunt, his mother's sister, had come to visit him, that although they hadn't seen one another in a long time, she had raised him.

"My real mother worked all day and went straight to sleep when she got home. Then, there was my aunt. I almost didn't recognize her."

He reached out, handing me the mate. I filled it up for me.

"I had to do a double take before I realized it was her. She didn't visit me at home, but at the precinct."

At the word "precinct," I choked on my mate. What was I getting myself into? He asked if I was all right, and I dodged the question. I'm not sure if he noticed, but he didn't comment. He had to wait for me to nod before going on.

"It was hard to get my aunt to calm down and tell me what'd happened. My cousin María had been missing for six days. She'd left nursing school and never made it home. I was so shocked, I didn't know what to say."

The man fell quiet for a moment. He looked at me like he wanted an answer, but I didn't say a thing.

He said his aunt started laying into his colleagues. She said the cops and the commissioner hadn't lifted a finger, that they weren't looking for the girl. But he wasn't really listening. He was thinking of his cousin María, who he barely knew and hadn't seen since she was a girl, a little kid, a distant cousin he'd fallen out of touch with. But his aunt's pleading, the way she was bent on getting help any way she could, had brought back the memory of his cousin. María had wanted to be a nurse. He was going to help.

I listened to him talk but had nothing to say. It bugged me that it was blood that pushed him to look for her, not the girl. Any girl. He was the law, that was his job.

He said he started looking as soon as his aunt left the precinct.

"I thought it'd be easy, as a cop," he said, "but a lot happened."

I passed him another mate. I felt like he'd talked too much. I was done listening, but then he added:

"I realized I was on my own on this one."

He pulled a photo from his jacket. He wanted me to take it, but I told him to hold on to it and show it to me from where he sat.

I felt sorry for him, but that's just how it was. Everybody looked on their own.

I studied the photo in his hands, then I studied him. Something in the girl's smile and in his body made me think that this time things could be different, that I might get there early for once. I didn't want another Florensia. I was the one who chose to lie to Florensia's mom, her eyes trained on me. And the guilt was mine to carry. Maybe things could be different with this guy.

I pictured the other yokes telling him: "She'll be back, probably off with her boyfriend," and I got furious at him, at all of them.

I watched him handling the photo and thought of charging him a load of money to get him off my back, but then I remembered the girl.

"It'll cost you," I said without blinking.

Yokes got paid to look and do fuck-all. Why shouldn't I?

He gazed at me in silence. A shadow of cruelty seemed to cloud his face.

"I'll bring the cash tomorrow, if that's all right, then we'll head over to my aunt's."

"I'm not getting into no patrol car," I answered.

He laughed. I liked the look of his white, even teeth. But the face he pulled reminded me of all the little tykes in my neighborhood, and I kept a stern look on my face.

"I'll bike."

He shook his head no. So I said:

"This is what we'll do. We meet again tomorrow, but you only talk about her. Not a word about the precinct."

He smiled, nodded, and said:

"I'll come fetch you tomorrow, I'll bring my car. My name's Ezequiel."

The yoke gone, I went to the bathroom. Even though there was no one home, I closed the door so I could get a good look at myself in the mirror. I had changed too. I knew the next few days would be crazy. I wanted to remember my face as it was now, in case it somehow got lost in the coming madness and changed altogether. I switched off the light, walked out of the bathroom, collapsed on my bed, and went on sleeping.

'll come fetch you tomorrow, I'll bring my car," was the first thought that crossed my mind when I woke up.

It spells trouble, getting into a car with a cuff. I got up and tripped over some combat boots on the way to the bathroom. Walter had brought a girl home. His door was shut and I couldn't tell if he'd left for the shop or if he was still in bed. Better busy than not, seeing as I hadn't mentioned I wouldn't be around. I righted the boots and set one foot beside them. They fit. I'd never had combat boots like those before.

The girl wouldn't have left without her shoes. She must still be hanging in my brother's room.

I used the same foot to nudge the boots off to the side and continued to the bathroom. While I peed, I checked to see if Walter had showered, if he'd shaved or whatever. Nothing. The last thing I needed was for one of them to turn up when the yoke finally showed. I scrubbed my face and teeth. The towel was gone: that was on my brother.

I shook my hands dry and ran them through my hair. Back in my room, I tried to change without making a racket. I'd wait for the yoke at the gate, so he wouldn't have to come in. Where were my pants? I couldn't go out wearing shorts. I checked my dresser, nothing: a pair of leggings, more shorts. The floor was covered in dirty laundry. I'd have to do a wash soon. Maybe there were pants by the sofa. That's where I fell asleep most of the time, music sounding on the PlayStation. I hated when Walter cut the music. Still, he either turned it down or off when he got home. Then, I'd wake up at three or four a.m. and not fall asleep again till sunrise. Or later, if the cats were scrapping on the roof. The only way I could sleep through the night was with music.

I found a pair of jeans under the living room sofa. They were pretty clean. There was an empty beer bottle, too, and I left it where it was. I grabbed the pants, shook them out, and slipped them on. I found my kicks, my cell, my backpack. I was hungry but there was no time for food.

I walked outside. The sun shone real nice, making everything seem greener. I was into it. For a while, I forgot I was hungry. There was a scent not only of earth but of plants. I took deep breaths as I walked so that my body would soak up the smell. The last step to waking up. I went up to the gate. I'm not sure why I peered outside, I didn't know what kind of car he drove. I turned around and leaned against the gate. The lock stabbed into my back and forced me to stand upright. I stared at my house so hard I realized I found it difficult to leave that place. Unclear why. It's not like I was headed to the moon. Just to the house with the missing girl, and back.

"María's gone, María's missing," I said aloud then turned around.

The sun struck the path. A cat dashed across the fence and two dogs chased behind it tongues lolling.

"Slobbery idiots. Git!"

The dogs ran on and the cat, for a change, fled onto the roof. The dogs snuffled the trash on the corner.

It must be time. I put the key in the lock, opened the gate, and went out. I locked up again and stashed the keys in my backpack.

Minutes later, he arrived.

I climbed into his gray, new-smelling car and he drove off. Ezequiel, he said his name was. As I watched him drive, I had trouble picturing it. As far as I was concerned, he was just a yoke. Now and then he looked at me too, which was awkward 'cause he clearly didn't know what to say. Outside, the sun shone full. On a corner, a nipper tried to skip over a ditch but misjudged and landed with both feet in the scummy water. The mother, not far behind him, conked him on the head and the brat burst into tears. As I watched them, I thought of the boy's head stinging from the blow, his feet wet from dirty water, of how pissed he must feel about bungling his leap. That's how I felt in that car.

"Music?" the yoke asked, like he knew.

I righted myself, switched on the radio. I scanned several stations and found nothing worthwhile. Then I hit on a Gilda song. Mamá had liked Gilda. She was always telling me about how Gilda had been a kindergarten teacher. I shut my eyes and pictured my old lady humming around the house. The only time I ever saw her happy was with music on and my old man out. There, on that mission I didn't want to go on, my old lady came to me in the voice of a kindergarten teacher who sang with a red-lipped smile and made it all the more bearable.

When the song ended, the yoke said "Thanks" and I opened my eyes. I laughed.

"You like Gilda too?"

"Thank you for coming all this way to do this," he said.

Suddenly, he didn't look that much like a yoke anymore. I tried to think of him as Ezequiel. His name.

"I'm hungry," I said, "but I can't eat right now anyway."

He said nothing, kept driving. I thought he'd gone somewhere else, that he didn't care what I had to say. But then he pulled up to the curb and came out with:

"See that?"

He pointed at something outside, on his end of the car. I craned my neck to read the sign: GRILLED MEAT PASTA FRIES. Leaning over, I caught a whiff of a scent that went straight to my head. I don't know if it was the deodorant he wore or some hair product, but I liked it so much it made me smile. I sat back down.

"You do your job and we'll come here after. There's no rush." Ezequiel smiled too.

He started the car. My feet didn't feel wet anymore.

María's house was pretty. Way prettier than mine, anyhow. I didn't know where we were and didn't care to ask. Ezequiel and his aunt looked my way like they were expecting me to say something and I, not knowing what to say, peered out the window at the grass, at the earth.

Then, the woman told me her daughter used to take her mate outside while she read over photocopies from nursing school. The woman nearly burst into tears. I told Ezequiel to stay there with his aunt and walked out. The door was ajar and I only had to push open the screen door, which was heavier than it looked.

Their property was smaller than mine, but nothing grew freely there. The grass was mown and weedless. The plants, small in their pots and flowerbeds, barely grazed my knees. I started round the house, questing for something, I'm not sure what.

I felt the screen door open and close, then saw Ezequiel and his aunt headed my way.

"Come, I'll show you," she said. And then: "Here. This is where my little girl used to study and drink mate."

She pointed at a spot on the property not unlike the rest, save for a chopped tree trunk hemmed by taller grass. I shifted the trunk, uncovering a couple of pill bugs and a centipede that scuttered away. The trunk was upturned; once against the earth, its damp side now faced the sun. There were a few live critters there too, unmoving, stunned by the unexpected light.

Beneath, stripped of green, was earth.

I asked them to leave, and waited. No one would ever watch me eat dirt again. I stood motionless till I heard the screen door close shut. Alone, I could slip off my shoes, sit down, rake my hand through the earth and feel it on my legs; for a moment, returning my body to its own. I didn't shut my eyes but conjured the photo Ezequiel had shown me of María. A lovely, black-haired girl. Beautiful when she smiled. I thought of her patients, glad to be touched by a girl like that.

The earth is always cold at first. But in my hand and, later, in my mouth, it grows hot.

I set some aside, gathered it up. Brought it to my mouth and swallowed. I shut my eyes, feeling the earth warm up and scorch me inside, then ate some more. Earth was the poison that would carry me to María's body, where I needed to be.

I lay on the ground, eyes shut. I had learned darkness could birth forms. I tried to make them out, to think of nothing else, not even the pain radiating from my stomach. Nothing but a glimmer where I focused my gaze till it turned into two black eyes. And gradually, as if crafted by the night, I saw María's face, her shoulders, hair born of the deepest darkness I had ever seen.

Thankfully, the earth didn't hug her body. She wore a pale dress over her skin, which made her look younger. She lay somewhere. Alive.

But there was something else, too: confinement. Light didn't enter freely where she was. María breathed, fearfully. No part of her smiled. The dress, which started at her shoulders, was lost in a clutch of blankets that appeared to trap her.

María gazed at me. Her face, a keen of sadness. Pain radiated from her black eyes.

As I watched her, I remembered my aching stomach. But I wasn't ready to return to my body. I concentrated on her and tried to stay, to figure out where she was. But there was only darkness. On the back wall behind the bed where María stared out at me were words I couldn't read. Could I read at all? Not in dreams. The letters went strange. Restless. By the time I grasped one word, the next had changed. It was almost impossible to read in dreams.

I crashed head-on into her body, which put me in a shitty mood. I couldn't move beyond that room to the place where her open eyes were, with a dread that hurt like a kicking. The pain came back, and my body returned to where it wasn't meant to be. I couldn't stay, it was agonizing, airless. I was so close to María, but it was no use.

Whenever I felt like leaving, I'd crash into her again. I wanted to move away, to look at her, feel her. Knowing she was alive, the pain mattered less. I gathered up all my strength so that I could break loose. I stopped looking her in the eyes so that I could move backward, farther, toward the wall and the words that, this time, I made no effort to read. Instead, I pretended to snap a photo of them with my cell phone. That's when I saw the phrase CARRY YOUR CROSS. A door instantly creaked open. I felt an intense fear. That was the last of it.

I opened my eyes.

I left the vision feeling breathless, as though I'd been locked up with her for days.

I struggled up. I was thirsty. My throat and mouth, parched. I felt dizzy. The thirst made me dumb.

"Water," I croaked as I saw Ezequiel walking toward me.

The woman strode behind him.

"Water," I said again. Then, mouth dying of thirst: "She's alive."

They led me to the bathroom. I shut the door on them. I guzzled down water with the same compulsion as I had during recess back when Señorita Ana used to look after us and tap water was the tastiest thing in the world.

I sought my reflection in the mirror and in it found something I already knew: *I'm like her*, I said to myself. *I know her name and I know she's alive. I want to find her. I look like María. My lips, my hair. There's earth in the color of my skin, and some of María too: eyes like a knife wound in flesh. I won't leave her there, alive, forgotten among shadows.*

F ries, lots of them. And a milanesa. Got any?"

I ordered my favorite food, the same meal I had every birthday. Back in the day, I used get out of bed and put shoes on so no one would scold me, then leave my room to look for my old lady.

The faucet would be on all the way, the water crashing down on a dark mountain of potatoes. The water turned the dirt to mud and then into a clouded river that flowed toward the kitchen drain. I used to be a pro at peeling potatoes with nothing but a Tramontina knife, but I never touched them on my birthday. "I'll do it," my old lady would say, nudging me out of the way with her arm. But seconds later there I would be again. I liked to see the potatoes all chopped up, to watch them frying. To smell them.

Milanesas, one each. Sometimes, when our old man wasn't home in time for dinner, Mamá would set his milanesa aside on a plate between two squares of paper towel. Not the fries, though. "Screw him," she'd say, and Walter and I would split our sides laughing. Those were the best birthdays ever.

Ezequiel ordered some sort of meat with a side of salad. Salad? That cracked me up. They sold all kinds of things in that joint and this john orders lettuce.

"To drink?" asked a straight-haired girl a year or so older than me as she took our order down in a notepad, not looking at us.

Ezequiel ordered a beer I'd never heard of. A dark beer from a weird brewery. They brought it stat, chilled. I loved everything about being there, about washing away the sadness of the earth in my body with beer and fries.

"You know we've got to go back, right?" said Ezequiel halfway through his beer.

I nodded yes. I was aware. María was alive but I didn't know how to figure out where she was. I didn't need to eat more earth to sense the dread in her open eyes. Her earth was still in my body.

"But right now I'm exhausted," I said, as they brought over a tray full of fries.

"I know. Let's eat. I'll drive you home."

I reached for a fry. I'd been brought a set of metal cutlery wrapped in a paper napkin. But I wanted to touch the potatoes. To sink my fingers into the platter. They were hot but not enough to burn my hand. I grabbed one, took a bite, and remembered the taste of thick-cut fries—so soft their insides were like mashed potatoes. Steam curled up from the fry, and I took another bite.

I was on cloud nine when Ezequiel said:

"I'll come fetch you tomorrow, I'll bring my car."

I didn't want to look at him. I went on reaching for fries.

That night I dreamed of Señorita Ana again. She seemed dimmer inside and wasn't even angry. Her sadness was bright, solitary. I walked up to her, and something inside Señorita Ana lit up when she saw me.

"I'm all alone here, you know? I can't go anywhere."

It was the opposite of my vision of María. Señorita Ana was in a vast, empty place. Forever on her own.

She looked much thinner and I couldn't tell if that was because she wasn't wearing her teacher's smock anymore.

The stench turned my stomach, and Señorita Ana looked at me with pity.

"The pain," she said, "it's not from here but from the earth in your belly."

I said nothing but wondered how much dirt I could scarf without wrecking my throat, my stomach, my body.

I thought to myself that I had to wake up. But I didn't want to leave Señorita Ana on her own.

"I've got to go. I'm sorry," I said.

This didn't make Señorita Ana angry either. She opened her arms and hugged me, then said:

"I know, I know. Hurry, Eartheater. María's still alive."

I was waiting for him.

The sun had just risen and I was waiting for him.

Walter was in his room again with the combat-boot girl. I'd heard them come in hours ago. I hadn't snuck a look. He must've fallen hard to bring the same girl home twice in a row.

The light outside was dim now and had started creeping into my room. And I was waiting for him. I knew Ezequiel wouldn't arrive that early, but I was awake and thinking about what we'd get up to. I wondered if, aside from going to María's house, aside from scarfing earth and, hopefully, finding the girl, he and I might do something. Which was stupid. Why was I thinking about that kind of thing?

Unable to sleep, I got up to shower. I went to the bathroom. The towels were missing again. What were my brother and that girl doing disappearing with all the towels? I liked the idea of hunting for one outside, of treading the soil a little before I had to leave. For some reason, I had the feeling I might not come back.

To reach the clothesline where the clothes hung to dry, I needed to stand by the side of the house. I took a few steps. The touch of the morning grass made me feel as though my feet would never fully leave that place. The ground got moister every day. I raked the grass with my toes so I could spy underneath. The earth was moist too. I touched it. Later, I would eat another woman's earth. Which was why, I thought, I was staring down at mine. Looking up, I saw him.

It wasn't even nine yet, and there he was, stood on the path. Ezequiel, watching me with that smile I loved. And me, a wreck—barefoot, disheveled, barely slept. I dashed into the house for the key to the padlock. I considered pulling some shoes on, but my feet were filthy . . . I had to let Ezequiel in as I was.

"Sorry," I said, opening the gate to let him through.

He followed me up to the house. I made a detour before going in, grabbed the first towel I saw and headed back. He followed me into the house and stood quietly in the living room, like he didn't know what to do. I gestured at the sofa and asked if he wanted some mate. Though he looked less awkward sitting down, he still gave the impression of carrying something inside that he couldn't let out. Pained, he didn't look like a yoke anymore. Just another joe.

"I was on my way to shower," I said, setting the warm kettle and mate on a chair for him, and slipping into the bathroom.

With Ezequiel waiting for me, I couldn't shower till the water ran out. The way I liked to. Piping hot water to douse my hair and coat it in shampoo. Water running over me and shampoo trickling down my body so I could take in its scent before rinsing off. I grabbed a handful of hair and brought it to my nose. Then, I sniffed my shoulder, the part of my body I liked best. I stood under the water a few more minutes. I crouched for the conditioner and as I reached for the bottle, noticed it was empty. Without conditioner, I couldn't brush my hair. I thought of the combat-boot girl and had the urge to murder Walter. Kid had never used conditioner in his life. I unscrewed the lid, filled it with water, screwed the lid back on, gave it a hard shake, stepped out of the water and emptied the bottle over my head, making sure to get my tips. I soaped myself. The water wasn't so hot anymore and I wasn't so happy with my shower. By the time I was done with the soap, the water was lukewarm. I stood under the shower a few seconds longer, then stepped out. I dried myself off with the towel I'd rescued from outside, a small one that barely covered my body. My hair was still drenched. I held the towel under the open faucet then hung it back on the hook beside the mirror, dripping wet. I took the lid off the bottle of conditioner and left it on the sink. Walter'd get the message. I dressed and left the bathroom.

Ezequiel looked like a statue. I hadn't expected him to drink any mate at all, yet he'd got through half the kettle. No sign of my brother or the girl. I sat, sipping mate. I'd hardly toweled myself dry and my hair was dribbling down my shirt. Sitting opposite a guy with a wet shirt on was starting to get on my nerves. I got up and said:

"Let's go."

"It's early, but we can ride around a bit."

I saw Ezequiel glance at the wet part of my shirt then look away. I leaned back to tie my hair up in a bun, a real high one, at the back of my head. I left the kettle and mate and headed to my room for something to wear over my wet tee, but on the way found tossed on the floor a light black jacket with buttons and red stripes that I really rated. I pulled it on, did up the buttons, turned around, and said:

"Ready."

I didn't want to eat anything before eating earth. We drove around in the car looking for something to nosh on later.

"Something sweet?" Ezequiel asked, and I couldn't help breaking into a wide smile.

The thought of dulce de leche made my mouth water. As did Ezequiel, his smell. I drank in his scent as he drove. I loved it. I tried to not look at him and to follow the road with my eyes, but his smell got in the way.

"Not long now," he said.

I closed my eyes and only opened them when Ezequiel stopped the car. I thought we'd arrived, but instead we were parked on a street corner in front of a huge bakery with a yellow façade. Ezequiel got out and walked across the front of the car. Seeing that I was still seated, he waved at me to follow.

We went in. I gawked at the delicious pastries, unsure what he'd pick. Instead, when our turn came, Ezequiel looked at me and asked:

"What're you into?"

Anything with chocolate and dulce de leche, I thought, and tried not to laugh.

I picked out heaps of pastries, especially the ones with icing sugar that made your mouth look like a clown's. I was sure all that food would last me at least three days.

At the register, Ezequiel paid an elderly, serious-looking man who handed him a bag with a picture of bread loaves on it.

Outside, Ezequiel passed me the bag. I was dying to open it. In the car, he told me to put it in the back. For later. I set it down carefully. I wasn't thinking of the earth anymore but about the pastries, like a boozy night out. About fifteen minutes later, we pulled up in front of María's house.

I didn't know her name. To me she was just María's mother, Ezequiel's aunt. She said she hadn't slept a wink and I understood her. I never slept the same again once I started eating earth for other people. The night before, I'd taken two beers from the fridge and left one, half-empty, by the sofa. As I drank, I had tried to focus on the music coming from the PlayStation. I wanted the beer to clear my mind. To not think of María tied up, María penned up. Nor of her mamá. And at some point, I had drifted off.

And there she was, María's mom, inching closer. I could tell she wanted to share something, but I wasn't interested. I was saving myself, fully, for the earth. Even so, she sat facing me and reached for my hands.

"Hija," she started, speaking more with her eyes than her mouth. "Daughter . . ."

I shook my head no. She stopped. But her eyes went on.

"No, that's not how it works," I said, trying not to look at her, trying not to revisit that barren time and those waifish years that chafed like sandpaper on skin and had made it so I could never again hear the word "daughter" from the mouth of another woman. "I've come to eat your daughter's earth," I said, and got up to go outside, alone, in search of a life.

I stroked the earth, which lent me fresh eyes and visions only I could see. I knew how much the crying of stolen bodies ached.

I stroked the earth, closed my fist, and with my hand lifted the key to the door through which María and so many other girls had passed, beloved daughters carved from the flesh of other women. I lifted the earth and swallowed it, then swallowed more, swallowed plenty, giving birth to fresh eyes that allowed me to see.

It was her. María's bruised eye was fire and fury in my heart, a mark that had not existed yesterday on her face of pure sadness. Drunk on earth, I kept eating. I needed to see. There she was, María. She grew agitated, as if sensing me. I tried to calm her. She jerked her two useless arms. María, tied to a bed that was pure filth to a body born goodness knew how many years ago—a handful, maybe seventeen. The bed rattled against the walls and María tugged and tugged at her bindings, scrappy rags that she couldn't break loose from.

Again, black letters on the wall of the cesspit imprisoning her. They shifted about, refused to be read. I crouched, but there was no earth to hold on to. I tried to curl my body into a ball, but my head, upraised, stared at María and at the wall behind her, black letters in darkness. She no longer struggled against her bindings. CARRY YOUR CROSS, I read, as though it was a photo.

The door by the bed swung open, the sound sheer terror to our ears. María's huge eyes were the only part of her not tied down, and they spoke to mine of fear, of being beaten, of the need to flee. I could barely make out the man entering the room. The light shot through the door like fire to our eyes. But I had to see him. I fought the light and, though it stung, glimpsed him: an old man, forehead outlined with sparse white hair, withered arms still strong. An elderly man, like one of those grandpas that hang around public squares, shaking María and saying: "Quiet, woman!"

I couldn't stand to see her cry. I had the urge to bite him. But I couldn't. I clasped my knees with my arms and the letters shifted then fluttered off the wall, black moths swooping down on me. The old man made toward me, too. Had he seen me? No. It was just the icy touch of fear, that same shock and pain in my belly.

I had to go.

Though I didn't want to, I left. Black as night, head thick with a black moth's borrowed flapping: CARRY YOUR CROSS.

The money in my pocket couldn't make me happy. I had tried with all my might and still failed. María might die that very night. Her mother had said only "come back" and, pulling my body to hers, placed a wad of money into hands dirty with her earth.

We drove in silence. Ezequiel looked sad too. Neither of us opened our mouths. I glanced at my hands. I hadn't washed them in the rush to leave. The strain not to cry had driven me out of the house. I took out the roll of notes fastened with a rubber band, studied it, and thought of how mad my old lady used to get whenever we handled money before a meal. "Wash that smut off your hands," she'd say, "it's full of germs."

My hands were filthier now than all the money in the world. I spread them so wide the pesos almost slipped between my legs. Ezequiel looked at me and said:

"Buy yourself something."

I didn't answer.

"You've earned it," he insisted. "Buy yourself something you've always wanted. Something just for you."

I replied by turning my head to stare out the window, as though doing so might sweep me away from that car and from that day, away from my dirty hands, my body, and the earth's spell.

Something for me, I thought. I thought of Walter's girl's jacket. The stuff we had at home was just there; we used it, period. I'd never had anything all my own.

A little later, we passed a street corner with a shop that sold towels and sheets.

"Stop here," I drawled when I saw it, but Ezequiel went on driving. "Stop here," I said, louder.

I got out of the car and strode to the store. It was nearly noon. The sun was clouded over and a chill was setting in. Though pretty, the jacket was flimsy and not the least bit warm. It was just for show. I reached the store, pushed open the door, and walked in.

The girl standing behind the counter didn't seem keen to help me.

"See something in the window you like?"

I hadn't seen the window.

"I want a big towel, just for me."

She eyed me like I was an alien, then snuck into the back. She came out carrying a whole stack.

"Towels," she said.

She set on the counter a pink one I didn't touch, then an earthy one—nuh-uh. The last towel was the dark purple color of a bottle of wine. I ran my hand along it, fingering it. Now that was a quality towel. I picked it up; it felt heavy. I tried it out, wrapped it around my body. I loved it.

I don't know what left the clerk colder, my hands grimy with dirt or the wad of money I pulled out of my pant pocket. Skeeved, she said, "It comes with this hand towel." I didn't give a damn about the hand towel but I said "all right" and the girl named a price that sounded fair. I unrolled the wad of money and started counting. Though she could see my soiled hands, I wasn't ashamed. I was focused on paying and leaving. Done, I handed the money to the girl. She hauled everything inside again. When she came back out, she was carrying a huge bag with a pink bow. I hated the bag at first, but then I thought to myself, *it's a gift, first gift I've bought myself with my own money*, and I liked that. I had a sudden urge to be home, to take a scalding hot shower and wash the muck and sadness off my body, then bundle it in that towel, a towel all my own.

Ezequiel was waiting outside. He glanced at the bag and smiled. Thankfully, he said nothing. We started toward the car. Though my eyes were down, something caught my attention.

I looked up very slightly and read the word "blacksmith" followed by the name, "Francisco," and a telephone number, all spelled out in twisted iron letters that formed a gate propped against a gray wall. The house was small and gray, the color of unfinished concrete, but the iron set it apart. For a second I pictured a man with a welding gun and one of those helmets that covers your whole head to keep fire from getting in your eyes. Above the gate, hanging on the wall, another message, drafted in the cruelty of iron: CARRY YOUR CROSS.

My heart fist-bumped inside my chest. I felt as though the invisible hand of a muscular man were squeezing my neck, strangling me.

I skidded to a stop on the sidewalk so that I could take in everything in front of that house. I read:

CARRY YOUR CROSS
AND I'LL CARRY MINE.

I couldn't get a word out.

A door creaked open where the weight of the metal met the walls. The wood was so old it snagged. A hand pushed it just enough to slip through. An old man emerged hefting some metal toward what looked like a garage entrance. It was him. After leaving the structure, the man stopped to catch his breath. He looked up and saw us. Though an iron gate separated us, he looked straight at me and then at Ezequiel. He smiled at him, stiffly, and immediately turned around and slipped through the door, shutting it behind him. His hand slammed the wood with a deep shudder. Something hung off the structure, a price tag maybe, but I couldn't read it. My eyes were fixed on the door. I thought he might come out again, that he'd gone back for something. The thought of seeing him again filled me with panic.

Everything felt impossible, like in a dream. I shifted my eyes from the wood doors, visible through the iron grate, to Ezequiel. I raised my arm and pointed at the door. Only then was I able to speak.

"María is in there."

hadn't thought he was armed, but the last thing I saw was Ezequiel on his cell phone with a gun in his hand. For days, I'd been driving around with a guy and his piece, oblivious to it. I clasped the bag of towels so hard the ribbon dropped to the ground. I trampled it, the muck from my shoes turning the pink bow the color of mud. I took a few steps back and glanced at Ezequiel. He wasn't looking at me, as though I had stopped existing the moment I gave him what he wanted. And right in front of the house of the old man who had stolen the girl.

I took a couple more steps back, enough to get off the sidewalk. I wanted to go home. Ezequiel raised his voice on the phone. The hand that held his cell moved with the same ease as the one holding his piece.

I rarely left my barrio, so I didn't know my way home from there. I'd let myself be swept along to help a man who was armed and a woman I didn't know. I turned around and started walking. I walked faster and faster. Hearing Ezequiel call me, I bolted.

I covered the ten blocks from the corner of the street to María's house as though I was running on air. I wasn't thinking about Ezequiel or the other yokes, or of what was about to happen. Just about my house and wanting to go home.

María's mother opened the door and, seeing me like that, clammy and breathless, rushed toward me. She frightened me. I opened my mouth. I tried to speak and say something, to explain the impossible to her, but in the end there was no need. Sirens from a fleet of patrol cars zoomed past her house and drowned out my voice, which never sounded. Seconds later, María's mother was no longer in front of me, shaking me to get me to say something. She was sprinting down the sidewalk after the patrol cars.

The neighbors' doors creaked open as they each came outside to see what was going on. I went in through the door left wide open by María's mamá.

It was night by the time Ezequiel got back. His faced was bruised. He had bled and his blood was now dry. I saw him come in and said nothing. He came alone, without María's mamá. I'd been waiting for hours. Restless from nerves. Head aching and stomach on fire. He came to me quietly, and his closeness surprised me. He hugged me. I felt the jolt of his body against mine.

"Thank you," Ezequiel said. "María's alive."

He held me a long time. I couldn't move without saying something. And I didn't want to. Everything was perfect. His embrace healed my body. My stomach and my head stopped aching. I no longer felt fear. I felt nothing. I don't know how long this lasted. Ezequiel said thank you again and, before letting me go, I thought I felt him breathe in the smell of my hair. I don't know why but my only thought was that he wasn't much older than my brother. They were probably the same age.

"Let's get you home. I'll drive you," he said, and I went to the kitchen for the bag of towels.

Señorita Ana came to me on nights I slept without waking.

In my dreams, below the sign she was found under and over earth made electric by the acrid light that exuded off bones turning to dust, Señorita Ana rotted like flesh off a dead dog on the road. Her bones weren't meek like domesticated animals. They stalked me and their fury contained the devastating force of those who seek justice.

I don't know why she seemed this way to me that night, like a dead woman with glimmering remains. After all, the police had found her body and taken it away when I was a little girl.

I rubbed my eyes.

There she was, again.

"Have you forgotten me? When will you be back to eat earth for me, mi chiquita?"

I could never bring myself to eat the earth below Señorita Ana's flesh, even though I knew exactly where she'd been left. I wanted to remember her perfect and clean like a smock hung to dry outside my house on mornings of sunshine lost to me forever.

Ana opened her mouth. Time had marked her face. The anger she felt toward her killers hurt me and hurled me into the middle of my night, forcing me to stay asleep.

"I'm here, Eartheater, down here. When will you come eat earth for me?"

It was about ten days before María's mom visited. My brother wasn't home and neither was Ezequiel, who sometimes came by to tell me about his cousin: she was on the mend, she wasn't too sad, she was talking about going back to nursing school; and about the old man, who was in jail, and the neighbors, who'd tried to set his house on fire. The only other person there was Walter's girl, who, when she wasn't studying, did nothing, like me. Sometimes I got the urge to ask if she wanted to play on the PlayStation with me. But I was always too embarrassed. So, I'd put some music on and she'd inch closer to listen. Other times, she muttered stuff or read from a black binder scrawled all over in Liquid Paper. *Power 2 Youth* it said on the cover in big letters, which I assumed meant she must have friends.

One time I asked her what she was studying, and she said she was reading History for the remedial test. She read to me a while. She read a bunch of stuff and I listened 'cause I liked the sound of her voice. She wore a black jacket as flimsy as her other one. I bet she was freezing her ass off, though it looked pretty on her. Her long, loose-waved hair perfectly matched her dark clothes and red lips, which spoke to me of towns of people who only left the land they lived and worked on to go to war, to kill or be killed.

Her hair was knotted in the back. I'd noticed the knots the week before, and now there was a massive one. We were out of shampoo and all that other stuff, and for days we'd been washing our hair with laundry detergent.

I thought of Walter shut in his room with her, of them rolling around and making a mess of her hair as it rubbed against the mattress. I'd never had hair like hers, stunning. I said I was going out for food and left. Walter's girl stayed on the sofa, the open binder balanced on her crossed legs and her head down, eyes buried in her studies.

When I came back with a packet of patties, some buns, and a bottle of conditioner for Walter's girl, María's mother was waiting for me at the gate. Alone. Her daughter wasn't with her. I was grateful, for my own sake. I nodded hello and the woman greeted me with a wink. I undid the padlock, pushed the gate open, and we walked to the house. Walter's girl had fallen asleep curled up on the sofa. The closed binder beside her body.

"Here," I said in a loud voice.

She woke up and I handed her the conditioner, a huge bottle that cost me two hundred pesos. I left the bag with the patties and buns on the living room table. She grabbed the bottle, smiled, and said nothing. She took a pack of cigarettes from her jacket pocket and started smoking on the sofa. I was happy she was there with me. If María's mother had said I was some drug lord or the head of a human trafficking ring, Walter's girl would've stayed right where she was, puffing on her cigarette and watching the smoke draw pictures in the air, like she didn't give a damn.

But the woman just stood at the door and said "thank you." So calm she looked like a completely different person. Something in her eyes told me she was sleeping again. She pulled a wad of cash from her wallet, this one smaller than the last, and offered it to me. I thought of the hours I spent at her house waiting for María to be saved. Everything was clean and tidy except for the dining room table strewn with hundreds of photos of her daughter. This time, I said no. The woman didn't insist, slipping the bills back into her wallet. She thanked me again, as though she didn't know what else to do. I gave her my hand and thought she might cry when she took it. I felt sad. I didn't know if for her or for what had been done to María, or for my mamá, for Florensia, for Walter's girlfriend, or for me. I felt sad for all of them at once. Enormously sad.

I went with her to the gate and gave her a stiff kiss. She left along the sidewalk by my house, like so many others, never to return.

To me Señorita Ana was the prettiest. I had never seen a woman naked. Only dead.

Since I kept growing and Señorita Ana didn't, little by little we drew closer in age.

Sometimes we sat and chatted.

I never asked her: "Who took you away?" Though Ana was alive in my dreams, I was scared she might die if I mentioned that there.

But, once, as she sat beside me and talked, I bent down to collect some earth from underneath her and tasted it. Horrified, she stared at me. She said I was never to do that again, that it wasn't allowed. It was the sort of thing she always used to say. "Climbing the tree isn't allowed. You might fall." "Running isn't allowed. You might smash into something."

I laughed. But after I ate dream earth and saw what little I did, I knew Ana was right, I'd better not. There was probably a reason it wasn't allowed.

An odd bottle with a card and a phone number. Even though it was day and the sun was bright, when I picked it up and read it, I thought of a long, dark night. The bottle had appeared at the gate a few days ago. It was the color of water and of the earth inside it.

I didn't want to leave it in the garden, among the plants and the other bottles. I took it to my room and set it next to the bed. I liked giving it a shake and watching everything mix together, the earth settling at the bottom and the water on top. Like a game where things are tossed up but then fall in line on their own. Something simple. The sort of thing that's never happened to me.

But on the card was a girl's name, and I knew there was a story behind that name, a story I wouldn't like. If I didn't leave the bottle in the garden, I'd have to deal with it eventually: uncap it, taste it, dial that phone number as though by force, like I was somebody's mule. Then I could throw it away or put it back outside. But a girl's name. A name someone had chosen for her. That name, I couldn't forget.

The bottle sat in my room for a week. Till I decided to put an end to things once and for all, to taste it and see what happened. It might be nothing. There wasn't much earth after all. A little bit at the very bottom, the rest water. Who'd told them that drinking water also helped me see? That was the last thing I needed.

I shook it a little, uncapped it, gagged as I shut my eyes, then drank, hoping that the name would lead me to a blurred face.

I saw a cheerful girl sprint toward the water. It couldn't be the sea, there was no sand. There weren't houses or shacks or shanty barrios around it, like there were by the arroyo. All around I saw green, and the girl slipping into the water, smiling. But then her smile clouded as though she was drunk and her body thrashed as it sank, struggling to come back up. Hands, arms, and legs fought to get out of the water. The air vanished and she, the girl, was forgotten at the bottom of the water, which blotted her from my eyes. Before I opened them again—my eyes stung—I thought of how alike they were: the night and the watery depths.

Didn't think you'd call," said a guy on the other end of the
line.

"Where is it?" I asked.

At first he was quiet, like he'd been taken off guard, but then
he went on to say he lived by Congreso and could come collect
me if I wanted. Save myself a trip. I cut in:

"Kid, where'd your girlfriend end up?" And when he said
nothing, added: "Besides, I don't leave my house."

The kid was fast, got there in under two hours. In my suite,
he said:

"Paraná de las Palmas and Paraná Miní, in Tigre."

He said they knew the place like the back of their hands,
they'd been going for three years and it felt like home. That's
what had got them lost, 'cause after she threw herself in the water
she never came back. He said his girlfriend had wanted to move
there someday. He spoke of how beautiful the river was, so wide
the trees shot up from the water. He said the handful of neigh-

bors on the island, and the police, and the tactical divers had all searched for her.

I must've looked like I didn't understand, 'cause the kid went on to explain that tactical divers were the ones who swam the riverbed in search of bodies, by touch rather than sight. It made me sad to think of living hands reaching out to touch some part of the girl I'd seen jumping and smiling. Which was why I needed to go there. I'd tasted the earth and the water I'd been brought and another bottle would make no difference.

"I need to see where your girlfriend jumped. My brother's got a motorbike, he can take me."

"Can't get there by bike. It's an island, part of the journey's by boat."

I settled into the chair, my body thrown back, and eyed him in silence. I was starting to regret my snap decision to help. As if sensing this, he said:

"There's a ferry, takes plenty of people. You don't have to go on your own."

The kid probably talked for another hour, trying to sway me. Then he left, a little down in the mouth, thinking he'd come for nothing.

My brother swung by for some tools and caught me on my own, legs lolling off the armrest, eyes fixed on my bare foot. He asked why I was lying around like that. And I said that I was lying around 'cause I didn't know how to get the river to give something back. That what the earth had told me wasn't enough.

He looked at me and said: why not see a mãe-de-santo? Then he left for the shop.

Not a bad idea, I thought. It would do me some good to ask and learn. I glanced at the bottle at the foot of the chair, my cell beside it, and closed my eyes so I could see the girl again, smiling. What could I do to get her back?

I picked up my phone and dialed Ezequiel.

The house was almost entirely white.

"Cheer up, kid," said red lips, and I felt as though one of those botanica figurines was walking toward me in bare feet. "You're a bruja, too."

And she laughed. She was around fifty, black-haired and big-bodied, as if some awful force had needed her firm flesh to hang comfortably. A colorful beaded necklace fell down her white dress, splitting it in two. Her hair, almost as long as mine, moved to the might of her hips.

Inside, the suffocating warmth of candles and a thick, incense-like smoke. The door shut behind me. On one of the walls, painted women walked into the distance with their backs to the water, leaving behind them gold prints in the sand. They looked like goddesses, and I liked that. I stared at them and, for some reason, thought of my body, picturing it in one of those dresses. The thought tickled me. I was a scrawny thing, not fit for a goddess.

Though I couldn't hear or see anyone else, I knew the mãe wasn't alone. I tried not to seem frightened. I remembered what the boy had said:

"Instead of looking for her, like I did every afternoon when I got out of school, I followed the river current."

I got up the courage and looked her dead-on. She smiled and said:

"I'm mãe Sandra. What brings you here?"

Kid showed us the way there. I listened as he gave directions to Ezequiel, listing a bunch of places I'd never heard of. Once he was done, Ezequiel signaled for us to get in the car. We said goodbye and drove off.

"Tigre," we were on our way to Tigre. I liked the sound of that name. Unlike "island," which I didn't rate at all: you need help from others to leave an island.

We crossed the city in silence and got on the highway. Ezequiel seemed to notice I was nervous 'cause he told me to put some music on if I liked, that I could have anything I wanted that day. He made me laugh.

"Anything I want?"

I turned the radio to a cumbia station and though he tried to fake it, I could tell it was torture for him. I stared out the window. I could feel myself getting sleepy, but couldn't take my eyes off the road.

"You've got to go. The river wants a body," the mãe had said. "Your journey there will be good. But not your arrival. There are forces working against you that do not want to welcome you. They'll be waiting, but don't worry. You'll do good."

The mãe glanced at me and I glimpsed something in her eyes. She stopped laughing. Her silence was grating. I felt as if she was rooting inside me for something. Then, though I jerked back, she lay her hand on my head. Caught it beneath her palm like a bug, and I was trapped. Time passed; I don't know how long. She released me with a faint smile. I was exhausted, as though years had passed in that one wordless moment. But it hadn't been long and I didn't know what had happened. I just knew something had.

Ezequiel was quiet, his eyes staring ahead. The faster we drove, the sleepier I got. I put my seat back and lay down. All I could see now was the car roof, the window, and the sky, a couple of clouds drifting slowly in the distance.

I wondered if we were being watched from above too, like the mãe had said.

At some point, I fell asleep.

When I woke up, Ezequiel was smoking through the open window. It took me a second to realize the car was parked. I rolled down the window and a sharp smell like wet earth wafted in. But wetter, watery. It was time for the ferry ride.

We got out. Ezequiel locked the car and I glanced at the river. A cold wind blew in from the riverbank like it wanted to knock us over. It stung our lips. Still, there was no way not to watch the water.

The ferry wasn't what I'd imagined. It looked more like one of those cheap buses people took to La Salada market, except tossed on the water. Ezequiel called me. We had to get going. The boat was waiting. *Whatever. Let it wait*, I thought. But we climbed on and sat by the window, facing one another. The boat was packed. Moments later, it pulled out.

Though I liked the color green, too much of it was draining. I tried to watch the islands passing us but my eyes drifted to Ezequiel. He wore sunglasses. He was looking at the view, and I was looking at him. His hair, his shades, his nose, his mouth, his neck, even the shirt he wore. I loved all of it. *How stupid of me*, I thought. I should've asked the mãe what the deal was with this dude. I chuckled to myself.

He asked what was up. *What do I know* I shrugged and inched closer. Behind dark lenses, I glimpsed his eyes and, on his mouth, a wide smile. We stared at each other for the rest of the ferry ride. I could smell the same scent on him as when he'd driven me in his car the first time. My mouth watered.

Half an hour later, we reached our island.

"We're here," Ezequiel said, getting up.

We edged across some wood planks and treaded land again. I was grateful for the earth, sturdy beneath my feet. The ferry left and we were alone. Ezequiel strolled off somewhere I didn't see, and I was left hanging by the riverbank, eyeing the water and hoping absurdly that I might learn something just by looking at it. I stared but couldn't hold on to a thing. The river changed constantly.

I felt someone calling for me. Ezequiel, waving. I turned to face the water and started down the island's edge. There was tar-black soil visible on the fringes, covered in grass and muddled with roots like worms. Strange as it may seem, knowing I couldn't eat it made me sad. But I wasn't there for that. I already knew what had happened here.

As I walked, I tried to picture the place where the girl had jumped, but Ezequiel kept calling and waving from a clearing among trees and large-leaved plants, so I headed toward him. As I drew near, dodging branches and bushes, a couple of cabins came into view. Raised on large wood stilts, they reminded me of the ones by the arroyo, except bougie.

I stood opposite him and before he could open his mouth, asked:

"Do you know how to swim?"

Ezequiel laughed. He said he knew how to swim, 'cause they were all forced to learn at the pig academy. I liked that he put it like that for me, "pig." And I thought of how he didn't seem like one to me when we were alone.

W e'd been waiting a while for the girl's boyfriend, who still hadn't arrived. I needed him to show me exactly where she had gone under.

Ezequiel acted like it didn't matter, but he kept chain-smoking. As night fell, the insects got noisier and the air cold.

We sat on the wood flooring around the cabin. Ezequiel said that he'd turn up any moment now. I didn't say a thing, but I had the feeling we were going to spend the night there. It was too late for the guy to show. I was thirsty for beer. I asked Ezequiel if he could get me one and he said he'd had the same thought. It was no use though.

"What do you mean it's no use? I want a beer," I said. He looked me in the eyes and smiled a brand-new, cocky sort of smile. He'd find me one, he said, and be right back.

I sat around a while, my back against the wood wall, doing nothing but listen to the insects, which were all over the place now. I watched a bug with weird feelers slowly make its way across the floorboard toward my white shoes. I hated bugs. I pulled up my shirt collar and had a whiff. Now that, I liked. I'd showered that morning, like I'd seen it coming.

I felt cold and went into the cabin. The bed stood in the middle of the room. It was massive and made up with nice sheets and a blanket the color of bare brick. I sat on the edge, watching the door Ezequiel would walk through with the beer. Crossing my legs, I started undoing my shoelaces.

The first thing he did when he came back was stroke my head. I swatted his hand away.

"Stop pretending to be a gentleman," I said and we laughed.

Ezequiel draped his jacket on the chair next to the bed. He handed me a beer and I sat up to drink it, covering my naked body with a blanket. We looked at one another. I didn't want to smile. I didn't want to make it too easy for him. He pulled off his sweater and drew close to me again. I didn't pass the beer. He grabbed it, took a long swill, and set it on the bedside table. The bottle hit the lamp and for a moment the only source of light in the room flickered. Just then, Ezequiel held the back of my head and kissed me with a mouth that tasted of beer.

His hand on my hair pressed me toward him while he drew me to his body by my bare waist. His hand felt rough, or maybe it just seemed that way to me, dizzied as I was by the booze and by his soft-lipped kiss. No part of him loosened its grip on me. I let myself be pulled toward him. His clothes felt cold. I wasn't even wearing my thong anymore, so I tugged at his shirt, which was impossible to remove in the position we were in.

Our mouths drew apart. We laughed some more.

Ezequiel quickly pulled off his shirt and his hand returned to my scalp. I leaned back a little, resting my weight on my elbows, and he laughed again. Undoing his belt and zipper with his free hand, he edged down his pants. His other hand held the nape of my neck. I couldn't move. He tugged at me. He pulled his cock out over his boxers and brought it to my mouth. I was drawn into a kiss so soft it was like kissing a tongue. I pulled his boxers off all the way. I liked the feel of his skin, which I clasped with my lips as his cock danced in my mouth, sinking deeper. Ezequiel watched me suck him off, and I watched him. He gripped my head with both hands and held them there for a moment. Then in a single motion, he pulled his cock out of my mouth and chased my waist with his hands, pulling me toward him.

I lay down and spread my legs. Ezequiel kissed my tits, the size of closed fists. His mouth still at my chest, he took one hand to my pussy. He stroked me. His fingers were fire. I got wet. He carried on a while longer, then grabbed my hips again.

He held me firmly with both hands, one dry, one wet. I wanted to watch him enter me. I wanted to stroke his back, suspended above my body. For a moment, Ezequiel looked me in the eyes. Then, slowly, his eyes and mine drifted apart. I didn't see him thrust into me or press against me or grab my ass hard with both hands and thrust again.

I could hear us with my eyes closed and feel the moment Ezequiel moved his moist hand from the top of my ass into my mouth, his body thrusting and shuddering violently as though he'd lost control. My heart went haywire and I pressed myself against him. Something deep inside me toppled. On his fingers, against my tongue, I could taste my own body.

Though early, the sun had risen a while ago and was in full view.

Everyone had gone on about the beauty of those islands and their growth, the vastness of the river. But it smelled musty to me. Like backwater.

The river, hemmed in, refused to give her back. It hid her away like the night hides its creatures.

We knew exactly where she'd jumped. Her boyfriend had turned up early on the ferry. He arrived, showed us the spot, then left as fast as he could, like he didn't want to spend another second there.

We were alone again, Ezequiel, the river, and me. The three of us headed in the same direction now, studying our steps.

"I love you," Ezequiel had said the night before. With my hair blanketing my face and his cock inside me, I stayed quiet.

I was walking to the island edge now, thinking of the girl. Ezequiel had stayed behind and quietly followed me with his eyes as he let me do my thing.

I sped up. I didn't think things would turn out bad. I wasn't thinking of later.

"It's one thing for another," mãe Sandra had said.

I turned around, looked at him, and he saw something in me that spurred him to follow.

It was just one thing for another, sure, but that goddamned river wasn't after flowers, or blood, or lit candles. It was after something else.

The thought scared me, so I stopped thinking. I let my body take the lead. I just hoped Ezequiel actually knew how to swim.

One thing for another. Getting back what was left of the girl was going to be like heading to the kiosk, handing over money, and getting something in return.

I was miffed.

I turned one last time to make sure Ezequiel was following, then I stopped thinking. I ran, leaped, lunged into the river.

It was like a trance, something swept me away. I don't know how long it lasted or what happened exactly; it was like falling asleep in the watery depths. I was enjoying resting there, feeling the fresh water seep into my body like a drug, but he pulled me out.

When I woke up, I was in a bed. Not mine or the cabin's, nor any bed I knew. Ezequiel was there. At first I didn't speak or listen to him, but I could tell he was there. I could smell him. I could feel him move as he tried not to make noise. He wasn't your garden-variety pig; he was a pig who looked after me.

I stayed still, eyes shut. The sheets were stiff and scratchy like cardboard between legs deader than I was. I didn't want anyone to talk to me yet. Through my eyelids, I felt the light. A light for sick people.

I wanted out of that shithole.

Ezequiel had pulled me from the river. Saved me. I wanted to know now what'd become of the river girl. If there was any news.

But I wasn't ready to open my eyes, much less my mouth. My head was still full of rushing water and bitter cold.

I opened my eyes. Again, light. Ezequiel saw me and came up to me, placed his hand on my arm. I wanted to tell him I was fine, that we'd better leave that dump, that I wanted to go home, but most of all I wanted to tell him that I wanted him, but I couldn't make a sound.

"It's over," he assured me. "The body showed up this morning. Drowned."

"Drowned," he said, and the cold returned.

I stopped trying to talk. I relaxed my body, let my head fall on the pillow. Shut my eyes. Drowned. It was all true. But it felt like too little. I saw red. Drowned.

After I ate earth in her dream, Ana went strange. She was leery of me. I tried to chat as usual, but it wasn't the same. There was silence. She studied my every move, and I felt as though she was keeping an eye on me, out of fear I'd eat earth again.

One time she said:

"I know you jumped in the river. It isn't allowed."

She looked pissed. She waited for an answer but not knowing what to say, I kept my lips sealed and my eyes on the ground.

She came at me, grabbed my hand, and dragged me somewhere I hadn't been before. Down a path I didn't recognize. Till I saw the sign: PANDA JUNKYARD.

I thought we'd stop there, where she'd been found, her body naked and splayed like a frog staked to the ground. But no, we kept going till we reached the warehouse, a couple meters away.

There was a door. Scared, I prayed it was locked. But Ana shoved it open.

I didn't want to go inside. I'd never felt so afraid in a dream. I wanted to wake up but couldn't.

Ana looked possessed. I begged her to let go but she hauled me to the open door. She told me to have a look, and I glanced inside. I saw a hand holding a knife. My heart lurched. I shook so hard I had to grab onto the door frame. Even with eyes shut I could still see a man's veiny hand gripping a knife pointed at my brother.

I started to weep. I would've begged Ana to stop, except I couldn't speak. If we stayed a second longer, I thought, Walter was going to be stabbed.

"You're not allowed near Tito el Panda land. Got it?"

I woke up, wrists sore like I'd been cuffed.

I walked down the first of seven blocks to the train station. It was still early. Hanging outside the small houses were clothes folks had forgotten to bring in, dampened by the morning dew. My old lady never liked for us to be out and about so early. She said there were guys still on the prowl from the night before, and that they were the worst kind.

Yesterday, somebody had left a bottle with a printout of a smiling boy. "Dypi" it read, followed by an address, a phone number, and the question: had anyone seen him? Something in his smile told me he was still alive, so instead of scarfing earth, I decided to pay a visit.

When I left the house, it didn't look like rain. Not a drop had fallen and yet the sky had grown dark. I hurried to the corner. One block to go, then I'd take the diagonal street and cut through there. I could've gone down the street that ran parallel, which was faster, but I never liked it there: that was where they tossed out the dead roosters.

Those roosters were burned into my memory. At first folks had arranged them on street corners alongside red candles, corn, a whole display, but then they started wrapping them in black trash bags that didn't cover them properly, so that it was impossible not to see them: dried-up feet or a crest poking through, bringing to mind petals torn from a cranesbill.

The diagonal street was usually busy, and at the end was a block of silk floss trees. I'd been nuts about those trees ever since I was knee-high and used to slop around the mud after a storm, the ground a carpet of pink flowers that colored the muck and made it look beautiful to me and my brother.

I was almost at the boom gate when it started coming down hard. I sprinted, the scent of wet earth rising. I passed the tortilla stand, which closed on rainy days, its trestle and bench chained to the lamp post. Though I went as fast as I could, it wasn't fast enough. Then it hit me: no matter how much I ran, I wouldn't make the train.

I stopped at the railroad crossing. The rain, a beautiful curtain. On the other side of the tracks, beyond the curtain, I saw a boy walking toward me with a massive dog. We were alone: he and his dog on one side, me on the other. The train rushed past, and I glimpsed them in the second it took each car to pass, a blink between train cars. I heard the kid calling desperately for his dog. It'd got away from him and was threatening to dive under the train. The kid yelled at the dog to come back, but it wouldn't listen.

He's not gonna cross, I thought. *He's got to know he can't cross.*

Another train car hurtled past and the dog kept on trying. The kid got as close as he could without risking being pulled under the train. But the dog wouldn't let up. He was waiting for the right moment.

He's not gonna cross, I thought.

Another train car had barely passed when the dog spotted a wider opening and dove in.

I don't think half his body got through before the train snatched him. The dog was dead in under a second. The train left him crumpled, a few feet to the right of the track.

I waited for the train to pass and crossed the tracks. The kid knelt by the body, its head turned back owl-like in the rocks. There was no blood, but the dog's fur was like torn cotton. He must have been a beautiful creature.

"Why did you want to die?" the boy asked.

The rain fell so hard I was scared the boy wouldn't see the next train coming in the state he was in. I had to get out of there. I was out of time.

"It's over, kid. The train got him," I said in a last-ditch attempt to get him to stand up, but the boy carried on like he hadn't heard me.

"Why did you want to die?"

I walked off under the rain, which by then had left me sopping wet. I reached the ticket booth. Stuck to the window was the printout of Dypi, who was laughing so hard in the photograph that his cheeks dimpled. I once again had the feeling he was still alive. The man behind the glass looked asleep and I didn't want to wake him. *No ticket then*, I thought, and walked to the platform.

The only good thing about that trip was the train pulling up to the station half-empty so that I got a seat. I rested my head on the window and ran through the list of stations, timed the distance between each, and worked out how long the ride would be. I set an alarm on my cell phone and nodded off.

I couldn't even rest while asleep. I dreamed I opened the door to my house and took a few steps in, then stumbled on something hidden in the crud of the sidewalk. It was small and I had to crouch to get a good look. A tiny, fallen pigeon. It opened its beak but made no sound. I wanted to help, except I didn't know how. I just stared. The alarm rang a few minutes before we reached the station where I had to get off.

Though the rain had let up, the sky was still overcast. Rug rats messed about between puddles on the dirt road. There were no cars. I walked a couple more blocks to the address I was looking for. There was no doorbell, so I clapped my hands. A girl opened and I asked for Eloísa. A man came in and had me sit down.

"Eloísa's not home. Probably on her way now."

The man's eyes drooped.

On the sides of the property were woven wire fences like the ones around a soccer pitch, but in front, at the entrance, just three rows of thin wire strung between wood posts. Because the house sat in the middle, you could see everything. Every once in a while, I'd peer out to check for the doña. Resting against a post was a cage with a parrot in it. A caged parrot is as good as a dead parrot. *Bad luck*, I thought. And the parrot, as though hearing me, squawked: "Wino, wino, to bed with you, wino."

The old man looked like he wanted to crawl into a hole.

I pretended not to hear the bird. Every once in a while, I turned to watch a yellow horse chomping on some grass. I'd heard once that horses that color had a special name, but I could never remember what it was.

Soon two women turned up.

"Eloísa's a fucking mess. She's on the street all day looking for her kid. Last time I saw her, she'd wrapped herself up in trash bags to keep the rain off. She's losing her mind."

Beside us, the horse chomped grass like it was nothing.

One of them said:

"You've got to catch whoever took the kid."

The other nodded in agreement.

Then they pulled up a couple of stools to sit with us. Eloísa showed about a half hour later. She walked in, then stood eyeing us. All those people must've seemed strange to her. She hauled a couple of huge bags behind her. The ones she used to keep the rain off, I thought. But no: inside were printouts of Dipy's face. She'd been putting them up around the neighborhood.

The woman said her kid had been missing for twelve days. She said the cuffs had given her the brush-off. Searching the woman's eyes, I said:

"Doña, I've come to eat your earth."

The skinny gal who'd been playing dumb while eavesdropping on us brought out a plate of dirt they'd fixed up hell knows when. I grabbed a pinch, pressed it against the plate, lifted it, and put it in my mouth. I shut my eyes.

First thing I saw was Dipy driving the cart. Though the yellow horse clomped steadily, there was something wrong with the kid. He kept rubbing at the fly of his pants the way kids do when they've got to go to the bathroom but keep screwing around till they can't hold it in any longer.

Dipy needed to take a leak and pulled over next to some trees on the side of the road. Wanting to give the horse a break too, he unhitched it from the cart, patted it on the neck a couple of times, and gave it a good rub. The horse hoofed toward the grass. It took a couple of steps then stopped. Dipy stood and peed. He was ready to hit the road but the horse wouldn't listen. The boy rounded the beast to check what was wrong. Just then, spooked by something it saw, the horse kicked its back legs and cracked the boy on the head.

I opened my eyes, dizzied. My first thought was that they would beat the horse to death. I didn't want to be around for that.

"Señora, a word. Alone."

The woman looked at me and said:

"Let's step outside."

I explained the accident to Elisa. She said nothing. Just stared at the beast Dipy had taken with him on his rounds. The horse grazed, offering its neck to the sun breaking through the clouds. Again, I said: an accident. But Eloísa wouldn't listen and instead muttered:

"I'm gonna tell the other women not to let the kids out on their own. Someone might steal 'em."

Tears dribbled down her cheeks as she spoke.

I didn't want to talk anymore. I took the woman's hands; she refused to look at me. She said again:

"There's a man out there taking boys who go out on the cart on their own."

"I've got to go," I answered.

I said a quick goodbye to everybody then headed out of the shack. I didn't want to be the one to tell the abuelo; I didn't want to tell anybody. I walked down the dirt road. Pulled out my cell phone, called Ezequiel, and told him the boy's story. Let the cuffs handle it. Dipy was dead. Then I asked him to come by the house. I had to see him.

I'd been waiting for about a half hour by the time Ezequiel showed. He came in and started talking, but I was hardly listening.

"What's up with you?" he said, and he carried on talking, sending stuff my way that I couldn't connect with.

I made this clear by touching his cock over his pants and using my other hand to grab his fingers and bring them to my scalp. Only when I started stroking him did Ezequiel relax and smile. He held me, pressed me against him. I loved the smell of him. There was no one else home and it was like nothing mattered but us and our kissing. I kissed then licked his neck, which cleared my head. All of a sudden, his hands released me and undid the button on his jeans, unzipped his fly, pulled out his hard cock.

Blowing Ezequiel was like a game to me. As I ran my tongue down his shaft and kissed it, I thought of ice cream. Ezequiel let me mess around a bit then grabbed me by the hair and stood me up. His hands undid my pants and yanked them down, as though tearing them off, then bent me over the small sofa in my suite. Facedown, his fingers fondled the place where his cock would penetrate me. He stroked me for a long while, like we had all the time in the world. Above all, I felt his heat. It hurt when Ezequiel first thrust into me—a split-second of pain—but then he was moving inside me and I was going nuts.

Two nights later, I dreamed of Ana. It'd been a while. I was starting to think I would never dream of her again but there she was, asking if I was angry.

I didn't say.

She said she hadn't come earlier 'cause she'd thought I was mad. I lied and said I was happy to see her, that I wasn't pissed or anything.

Now I was the one who didn't trust her. She had asked me to taste her earth and, when I did, had lost her shit. I didn't want her yanking at my wrists either, like last time. But Ana was my friend, and I never wanted to lose her.

I said:

"Let's have a beer?"

"It isn't allowed," Ana answered, opening her eyes real wide.

And we both burst out laughing.

Even though I nearly always realized it was a dream, I never asked her: *Who took you?* But I thought about it more and more.

She didn't bring it up either, though I had a feeling she knew. And the thought of it made me ache.

That time I ate dream earth I saw a man drag Ana by the hair and heard an awful cackling sound. Everything but her had gone shadowy. The white of her body seemed to glow in the dark night and between dark hands that heaved her and tore off her clothes. Terror nipped at my spine and I had to stop watching. Seeing as she'd told me off afterward, I'd decided not to mention it.

We were silent.

In my dream, Ana had a small purse. She glanced at it and at me, then said it would've been her birthday. She asked if I knew and I shook my head. Then she opened her purse and pulled out a can of beer.

I eyed the can, a pitiful amount for the two of us, but she smiled so hard I didn't care.

"On birthdays," she said, "it's allowed."

And the can popped open with that sound I loved.

It was Friday evening. Ezequiel was on duty and would only visit on Sunday. Thinking of all the time left until I'd see him felt like walking blindfolded through La Salada. I sat on the suite sofa, got up, strolled around, sat back down; I couldn't stay still.

Walter and his buddies were pre-gaming in his room before heading out to El Rescate. Ever since the combat-boot girl had stopped staying over, my brother loved clubbing and being out all weekend. I wasn't about to stay home on my own, locked up.

Somebody knocked again. I got off the sofa to answer the door. Some of my brother's friends were like aliens. They'd come in and not even say hello, just "Where's Walter?" then "What about the games?" and head straight to his room.

But this time when I opened the door, one of them asked if I wanted a chocolate.

I laughed and said no.

Then he pulled something out of his pocket that I thought was chocolate but was actually a joint, offered it to me and said:

"Smoke?"

We sat at the door and lit up facing the weeds. The paper smelled chocolatey and let off a sweetish smoke as it burned. I spaced out watching the plants. Neither me nor my brother had tended to the garden and the passionflower looked ready to swallow the house. Most of the flowers had opened, though a couple of orange buds still hung around. Beyond the branches, my barrio stirred the way it does at nightfall. And I didn't mind thinking that one day, if Ezequiel, Walter, and me all went to shit, the passionflower would swallow up our crib like a carnivorous plant.

A house can die, too.

We took our time getting up and it was like stretching awake after a nap. We laughed across the suite. The kid stole into the room, and I went to the bathroom to splash my face. I didn't want to be alone. I had to work on Walter, so he'd let me come to El Rescate with them. I ran my still-damp hand over my hair, and try as I might I couldn't wipe away my smile. It was tattooed on.

When I walked into the room, the kid was sat with the rest of them on the floor. The room was mobbed.

"What're you up to?" I asked from the doorway.

Walter didn't answer.

Some kid I didn't know asked:

"Anything to drink?"

"Nothing, I don't think. We can grab some beers on the way to El Rescate. I've got cash," I said, glancing at my brother.

Walter peeled his eyes from the PlayStation for a second and looked at me.

"Fat chance," he spat out. "No way am I taking you."

His answer got me riled up. He hadn't even looked like he was listening!

I left the room and went to the kitchen for a drink. I opened the fridge, more out of habit than the hope that I would find something. I spotted two beers, snagged them, and grabbed two tankards from the cupboard. I walked back to the room balancing it all. As I nudged the door open with my foot, one of the beers slipped from my hand and smashed on the floor.

I smothered a laugh. The sight of those shards scattered all over filled some part of me with joy. I went to the kitchen for something to clean it up with and, on my way back, thought of my mamá. Mamá had been nuts about those fused glass animals. She used to buy them for peanuts at the market, and the colorful critters slowly took over the top of the fridge and the rest of the house. My old man started laying into her about it, asking why she kept burning money on that junk. Until one day he lost it and broke every single one of them. The day after, my old lady swept up all the pieces and put the little critters back together with Poxiran. I'd admire them now and then. No longer see-through, the brownish glue had turned them dark, like monsters.

The reason I was so tickled by that broken bottle, I thought as I swept glass into the dustbin, was because I was Mamá's daughter. Walter came into the kitchen, alone.

"Sis," he said, his hand on my shoulder. "Let's head out."

El Rescate was slammed.

Boys and girls passed each other plastic liter-cups of beer, hands held high like suns to keep them from spilling. The floor thumped to the beat of miniskirts. Just seconds after we got there, Walter melted into them like a zombie. I thought it was the music, but his eyes were lost in the colors of their skirts.

It isn't just love that makes the heart race, but music too.

Everybody smiled and reached for one another. Everybody touched and danced. Cigarette smoke curled up to the ceiling lights mixed with fumes that seemed to rise from the bodies.

I didn't expect to see anybody. But as I watched people hugging and cheering, I bumped right into Hernán.

"I've got an old lady now," he yelled so I could hear him. "Her name's Yésica."

Only after hearing her name could I picture Hernán, the boy I hadn't heard from in years, with another chick.

"We've got a two-year-old girl," he added.

Nearly knocked me on my ass. Hernán, in Dad pose, smiled and puffed out his chest.

It was nice seeing him again.

"You're not a brat who scares off anymore," I said, taking a long swill of beer.

I didn't want to but for a second my mind drifted to Ezequiel. Then I took another swig, emptying the cup, and had the urge to chase after the music and the other kids.

"Che, can you dance? Don't want some chick to come yank me by the hair!"

Now Hernán was the one laughing. He said Yésica was super chill and sure, he could dance, it was no big deal.

We started to move. To warm up. Hernán was dressed in black. Like me. We were the only ones there in black threads. On top of that, he wore a studded jacket with a picture of a skull, and the sides of his head were shaved down to his scalp. Though we stepped all over each other at first, we kept going.

Las manos arriba went the song, and everybody raised their hands and pumped them to the beat, like we were shooting the sky. I raised my hands too.

We danced a bunch. I didn't feel tired, just more and more fired up. After a while, Hernán said he had to go, that he was looking for cash to buy some kush, but he'd treat me to a beer first.

He went for the beer then came back. We drank to the side of the dance floor as we watched people move. I felt like a tourist; I'm not sure whether he did too.

"I'm sorry," he said at some point, his eyes glued to his cup. "I was scared."

Then he kissed me on the cheek and held me for a long time. He turned around and left. As I watched him make his way to the exit, I thought of that night, of the guy in the car and the gunshots. That was the last time we were together.

Just as he was about to fade into the crowd, Hernán turned around, raised his arm for one last wave, and vanished.

I hung about on my own for a while, till I was ready to go. My head was heavy with the crackling lyrics of cumbia but none of their joy. I felt out of it and my legs tingled.

I headed toward the exit. There was a long, tunnel-like hallway. I sauntered past it like I wasn't sure if I should leave. By the time I walked out of El Rescate, it was so late I couldn't tell if it was drizzling or if it was just the dew that falls before dawn. I was expecting to see the palm tree path that led to Route 8—two rows of slender palms squeezed between flagstones and revving trucks—but was instead blinded by floodlights and forced to shuffle forward with my eyes on the ground.

I walked like this for a few feet then gazed up, eyes squinting against the light. People darted around nervously, and farther ahead, a crowd formed around something as though around an accident. It was a drag, but there was no avoiding it. I sped forward, elbowing past so I could get ahead fast. I spotted some cuffs trying to hold people back and, farther off, someone lying on the ground in a puddle of blood. I inched closer for a look. First, I recognized the black studded jacket. Then the skull. And Hernán's face.

Somebody grabbed my wrist.

"What the fuck are you doing with this scum?"

It was Ezequiel. The look of disgust on his face when he saw me is still burned into my brain. I'd never heard him call us "scum" before.

Spewing with rage, Ezequiel grabbed my hand and pulled me across the barrier his partners were setting up. I don't know where he was planning to take me, but I tugged at his hand and stood my ground so he would know I wasn't going anywhere. I went back to Hernán. Pain buckled my knees, and I knelt beside his body.

"You know him?" Ezequiel asked.

I didn't answer but didn't let go of his hand either. I didn't even let it go when I reached out to stroke the earth and Hernán's body as though they were one. I let my hand fall beside the black jacket and stared at the skull patch to avoid looking at Hernán. Then I tore out some dry earth and broke it the way you tear a friend out of your life when they die.

I wanted to speak, whether to the earth or Hernán's body I wasn't sure. Instead I gripped Ezequiel's hand harder and got up.

I couldn't hear a thing. The other cuffs kept trying to fend off the rubberneckers, but it was hard going. They didn't want to leave. And I wanted to talk so much it burned my throat. The silence grated at my soul, and yet I wouldn't be able to eat earth if

I was busy talking. I was cold all over except for my hand, warm inside Ezequiel's. I stuffed my other hand in my pocket and gripped the earth like it was a piece of gold.

I noticed people looking at me. Had someone said, "Eartheater?"

I couldn't hear but I could see. A haze of eyes that gaped like holes. Behind running mascara and sleepless faces was a mix of pity and rage. And something new: fear.

Ezequiel got me out of there. He led me to his car, opened the passenger door, sat me down, and locked the door. I felt as though I could still feel their eyes on me.

"Wait here."

What were they afraid of?

Me?

Hernán had gotten away the first time. And now he was dead. He hadn't come back; I was the one who'd gone to meet him, without trying.

I waited for Ezequiel to get away from the car and shoved the clod in my mouth.

I knew it would hurt.

I screwed my eyes shut.

The darkness lasted only a moment.

Then I began to see.

I went to bed hungover. That had to be it. In my dream, Ana had dark rings under her eyes. I'd never seen her like that. She sounded unhinged.

"Panda Junkyard. Off-limits," she said, as though casting a spell.

Wanting to shut her up, I said I knew. She'd already told me.

But Ana didn't buy it. She looked at me with sad eyes and said:

"But you're gonna go. You're gonna go!"

She was out of her mind, unrecognizable.

"It wasn't just one person. One guy dragged me. Another tied me up. Loads more tore off my clothes."

I didn't want to hear it. I covered my ears and muttered *it's just a dream, a dream*, the pain boring into my head.

She went on. I couldn't keep track of the men she was naming.

I took my hands off my ears and Ana fell quiet.

She waited a beat and, once she saw I was listening again, pressed me:

"Panda Junkyard. Off-limits."

I woke up. I didn't want to dream of Ana ever again.

Her arms and legs were constantly moving. As were her lips, which spoke with the power to draw in every eye. Her flesh hugged her body, a tiny artifact with the pull of things shiny and new. She looked about thirteen to me, though I still hadn't decided if she was a girl or a boy. I needed her to speak louder; I hadn't slept enough and felt a bit lost. From where I stood, I couldn't make out her voice. What reached me was the laughter. "Miseria," they called her, and I thought she might blow a fuse. Instead, she just shat herself laughing, like it was nothing. Whenever someone said "Miseria," she owned it, like it was just another name.

When I woke up after midday, Walter was hanging around the same boys we'd hit El Rescate with the night before. And every one of them had brought a girl home from the dive. Someone— was it Walter?—had come with Miseria.

She's got to be a girl, I thought, my eyes—and everybody else's— glued on her.

Nearly everyone sat on the floor. A couple of kids were on the sofa in the suite. And Miseria stood dead center, yammering on and on.

My brother was in the kitchen serving Fernets. Every now and then he would bring us one. As he reached out a glass, someone's hand would take it and slowly bring it to their mouth, as though between each sip they became lost in some memory of Hernán.

Miseria was probably the only person who hadn't known Hernán. *Too young*, I thought. She was scrawny. Her hair barely covered her ears and was always coming loose, sweeping down by her smile.

Walter handed me a Fernet, and I sat on the floor. Though I drank slow, it hit me right away. I hadn't eaten. It was like the floor of our house was turning little by little into a bodiless wake. There were glasses passed from hand to hand, pockets of laughter, silence.

What were we gonna do?

I couldn't think of anything. I wanted to call Ezequiel. I wanted everybody to leave. If Ezequiel had come by and found us all drinking, he wouldn't have understood.

I folded my legs and hugged my knees on the floor. I was so wound up and lost in thought when Miseria started talking to me that I had trouble speaking up. She was slipping down next to me, asking if I minded.

That's when I realized everybody but me was with someone.

"All right," I said and she sat down.

She said she'd left her leggings in the club coat check. I said nothing. I was thinking about the fact that I hadn't said goodbye to Hernán, and that it was too late now. A girl started crying and someone hugged her and handed her a drink.

"That's why I'm wearing your brother's pants," said Miseria, letting out a loud laugh. "I look so lame."

She reminded me of myself.

"If you left your leggings in the coat check, what were you wearing when you left El Rescate?"

Miseria pinched two fingers, meaning something small.

"Just that, a yellow miniskirt, like the song," she said.

I smiled.

Miseria nodded and then told me she'd known Hernán since she was knee-high. When her old lady was out of work, she used to take her to a soup kitchen in the barrio. That's where the boys started calling her "Miseria."

"Let me read your hand," the ballsy brat said.

She didn't ask. Just grabbed it. As she studied it, I thought of how I used to go to soup kitchens too when I was a kid.

We had to eat everything with a spoon 'cause there were no forks or knives. We had to make do. A doña used to pass them out while looking us square in the face, and we'd hang our heads so as not to see the grimace that turned up on her cheek like a worm. I was frightened of her and did my best not to look at her. If she caught us eating with our hands, she'd rap them with a wooden spoon. "Animals," she'd say.

After Mamá died, Tía used to take Walter and me to that soup kitchen to have our bellies filled. And one day the doña had told me the same thing Miseria was laying on me now as she ogled my hand:

"Everything's gonna work out in the long run. Though you'll pay a huge price for it, you'll find your way eventually."

I kept smiling, not sure why, like I'd been bit by the *culebra del amor* Hernán and I had danced to the night before.

I stared at Walter as though trying to ask: "Where'd you find this one?" but my brother didn't get it. He kept handing out Fernets like they were medicine.

I took another sip and, again, thought: *What the hell are we gonna do?*

If I opened my mouth, everybody would want to tear into Ale Skin.

I first saw him a thousand years ago, though I remember it like it was yesterday. I was little, six or seven, and kept throwing tantrums, dead set on getting this pair of boots. Nobody paid me any mind. Until the afternoon of my birthday, when my old lady handed me a bag with a ribbon on it. I hadn't even opened it when she said:

"Don't get them dirty."

I was such a dumbass. I slipped them on straight away and went out on the street to show them off. Some little brat picked a fight with me and the other girls came out to back her. I couldn't hack it so I went inside. I wanted to take my new boots out for a spin—no way was I taking them off—so I decided to shadow Walter. I went to his room and waited a long time, till he was ready to head out. Walter wanted to hit the arcade. The old man pulled a face like he'd stepped in shit and spat out "bad crowd," but Walter didn't care.

That afternoon we were both dead set: me on my new boots and Walter on the arcade. And off we went.

We walked fast, eyes straight ahead, not talking. Walter suggested we go along the tracks. It was faster. I hated jumping the wire fence, but the advantage of the tracks was you didn't bump into anybody. I tried to jump over, like my brother, but couldn't. I crawled underneath it instead, not seeing the oil hidden in the burnt grass. It got right on my boots.

I wiped them, closed my eyes, then wiped them harder. But the stain was there to stay, and spread to everything I touched. I hugged my legs and started crying. Walter tried to comfort me so that I'd get up and cut it out already, but I only stopped after opening my eyes and seeing them striding down the abandoned tracks.

It wasn't their black clothes or skinheads, but the way they charged toward you that made you feel like they could grind you to dust. Ale Skin was the only one carrying a huge stick. My brother said "a baseball bat" and fear choked me. Instead of heading to the arcade, we stood there frozen stiff.

Once they had gotten near us, Ale Skin brandished the stick and said:

"I wanna play."

The other three laughed. They chatted and cackled right in front of us, like we weren't there. One of his buddies said "let's play with the girl's head" and Ale Skin swung the bat like he was gonna take my head off. Walter got in front of me, fast, and fixed his eyes on Skin. The other three laughed, and I nearly peed myself. Then, Skin dropped the bat, went up to my brother, and spat in his face. They laughed again. Walter didn't budge. Just as my heart was about to burst with fear, they turned around and walked away. I don't know why. Walter wiped his face with the sleeve of his sweatshirt, and we were silent.

In my vision, Ale Skin wore all black, his head shaved. Just like last time. But instead of a bat, tucked in his clothes was a knife. Which he used to end Hernán's life. Fast, barely goading him. Dude knew what he was doing, and I still didn't know why.

Miseria took a couple of sips of Fernet and handed me the glass. My hands were already shaky. I hated that I had spilled the Fernet. I hated the stains. I hated the booze sloshing on the floor of my house and the tears being shed on them for our dead friend.

It was Ale Skin, I thought. The words seared my throat but I didn't want to speak them: words can also stain you. I drank from the glass, now steady in my hand. My brother was the only one standing at the gathering, and I raised it to him. He raised his back.

Miseria glanced at me, smiling. She probably thought the Fernet had got to my head, that I was out of it. Then she pointed right between her ribs and said she had a stomachache.

"Have you eaten?" I asked.

First she shrugged her shoulders, like it didn't matter, then she shook her head and laughed. She stopped abruptly and touched her belly. She asked for the glass and took another sip of Fernet. Miseria was hungry and she was drinking Fernet. I wished I could say I'd fix something up for her, but there was no food in the house.

We were gonna have to go get something to eat, I thought, but herding that many people wouldn't be easy. I was having trouble getting going myself.

I struggled to my feet with my eyes fixed on Walter, busy chatting with two girls and a boy. I headed his way, thinking I'd suggest we get pizza, or some bread and cold cuts, but when I reached him my mind went blank and all I managed to come out with was:

"The earth said it was Ale Skin who killed Hernán."

Death-like silence, then everything exploded. The kids shot to their feet, furious, and started talking and screaming all at once.

No one listened.

"Motherfucking Ale Skin," said one.

"Motherfuckers. You know what we're gonna do?" said another.

"We've got to avenge Hernán," said a girl I didn't know.

They all talked at the same time, said the same thing over and over, and got more and more worked up. My brother was the only one not talking. He paced this way and that.

I thought: I should've called Ezequiel. Or, better yet: never gone to El Rescate or bumped into Hernán. I wanted them to go away. To leave me alone in my house. My head throbbed.

I scanned the room for Miseria, but she was gone.

I found her in the kitchen.

Leaning against the kitchen counter. Eating fries from a cardboard cone damp with grease. You could smell them from the doorway. She shoved them at me:

"Want some? Found them in the fridge."

I said I wasn't hungry and she carried on eating, lapping the oil off her fingers like she didn't give a shit I was there. She looked down, rooted around the bottom for the last fries, still chewing.

That's when Walter came in, clocked us, said nothing, and left. He looked out of it.

Miseria saw him leave, then looked at me, swallowed, and said:

"Bitch, why didn't you tell me?"

Not a soul left in the house.

Even heavy with booze, sadness, and exhaustion, the kids walked fast.

Not me. My mind was on the last few dreams I'd had of Ana, on Walter at Tito el Panda's, on the edge of the blade pointed at him. I knew it was the same one that had pierced Hernán's skin, and that we'd see it again. I thought of ringing Ezequiel. Or sending a text, at least. No. I'd have to waste hours explaining.

I glanced at the girls. A couple of them, glued to the boys, took massive steps to match their stride. No more roads or street noise. The reedbed rose into sight, and farther ahead, the piece of land I'd always been scared of, with trees and plants that looked like they hid people away.

We left familiar turf and entered another. One I didn't like at all; I knew that if I tried the earth there, it would show me stuff I didn't want to see. And throw it in my face. Like the air rushing us, which carried a different smell.

The others hurried faster and faster. And I followed. Miseria looked almost amused. She had no trouble keeping pace. She laughed, not even out of breath. Did Hernán matter to her? She made me a little mad. My brother and me, did we matter to her at all?

For better or worse, Miseria was with us.

She asked me how long we had left.

Not much, I said, and she stopped laughing.

"You ever been to this side?" I asked.

She opened her eyes wide and said:

"Hell no. What for? My old lady'd kill me."

The huge sign over the main warehouse was visible now. Though one side was eaten away by rust, you could still read: PANDA JUNKYARD.

We left it behind us. Ahead of me, a girl tripped and fell. The grass was tall, the ground invisible beneath it. Two boys helped her up as she gripped her ankle. She hobbled a little then started walking again. The rest of the group hadn't stopped. Neither had Miseria. Those of us lagging behind legged it to catch up with everyone. Now that we were closing in on the place, no one wanted to be alone, away from everyone else, when Ale Skin blew in.

Night fell.

A truck was parked across the parking lot entrance, its trailer filled with crates of beer, as though for a party. The folks ahead stopped to study the truck as they waited for us to catch up. I touched one of the bottles. It was hot. The ground beneath the truck was no longer earth but pavement.

Together, we shuffled toward the entrance of the lit warehouse.

Miseria and me looked at each other sidelong.

The joint would probably fill up later, considering the amount of booze they had on hand. It was still early for a Saturday night. The beers still hadn't been stocked in the fridge.

A hulk stood at the door.

"What's playing?" my brother asked.

He looked us up and down.

"You here for the matinée?"

Since none of us said anything or showed any signs of leaving, he studied us a while and then, in silence, shifted his massive heft out of the way to let us pass.

Place was a shithole. Darker inside than out. Night still fell, and the folks who'd been boozing for hours looked like zombies.

The ceiling was so tall, it dwarfed us. But I tried to keep my fear under wraps. A song I'd never heard was playing. The walls, once white, were now a cruddy gray, and the light, smothered in cigarette smoke, was dim. The smoke surprised me. I didn't remember it from my dream.

Out of all of us, Walter was the only one walking tall. We split into groups of two or three. Miseria headed toward a section with tables and I stood next to her. I couldn't turn my back to anyone. I peered around for a familiar face, but all I saw was a bunch of zombies. Now and then, the others glanced back at me.

Miseria's face was fixed in a smile, proof that everything was all right. But it was different from the smile she wore before. She was searching too. Like me, like everybody else. I was waiting for the first sign of what the earth had shown me. From that moment on, everything would come crashing down on us, unstoppable till the blade.

On the tables, between the glasses and bottles, were cards: colors, diamonds, hearts. The only women in that joint were Miseria, me, and the other girls who'd followed us. The rest of them, all men, didn't take their eyes off us.

We walked up to a table. The other players moved to make room. I didn't understand what they were playing, but the scent that wafted up from the table and the men's bodies and from the glasses and ashtrays filled with cigarette butts reminded me of the smell that had clung to my old man's clothes, hair, and skin. Some guy passed me a heavy glass. Before the glass, I felt the touch of his hot hand. I took a sip. Though I didn't recognize the flavor, I liked it and took another, longer swig, then handed it back.

I saw my brother walk toward a long bar lining one end of the warehouse, past the tables. Two of our people followed. He walked with a confidence that caught my attention. He leaned on the bar, ordered something, took the bottle of beer handed him and paid. Then he turned around and drank straight from the bottle. He never drank straight from the bottle when we went out. It bothered me. No one in there drank like that. He took a swig from the bottle again. Even the folks at the tables started glaring.

I walked up to him and said:

"Finish it, Walter."

Instead, as if not hearing me, he passed the bottle to the kid next to him, who drank from it without wiping first. They roared and started making a racket.

Everybody watched my brother and the two guys as they laughed and passed the beers from hand to hand. Until at some point Walter knocked one back, choked, and started sputtering. He tried to carry on drinking, but the coughing got in the way. Foam spilled from the bottle to the floor. Seeing this, my brother, still coughing, dropped the bottle and let it smash on the ground. Doubled over, he started puking.

Behind me, a prickly voice dripping with disdain. The same voice I'd heard the evening of the stained boots. The voice of Ale Skin.

"Look at what these barrio scum motherfuckers are doing."

Turns out I hadn't recognized Walter's hand in my dream. He swiveled to face Ale Skin and pulled out a blade like the thing had been on standby. The effect of the beer was gone. Walter was alert. He lunged at Ale Skin, who dodged him by a whisker.

Ale Skin pulled a knife from the back of his pants and turned to face him.

Other skinheads milled about too.

Miseria was shoving one of them around, come from hell knows where. She grabbed a bottle and I looked away. Next thing I knew, the bottle was broken and the guy on the floor.

Ale Skin shrugged off his jacket, eyes fixed on my brother. He was waiting for Walter to attack with his blade. And Walter was waiting for the moment Skin's knife would shift in his left hand: in his face, I saw something animal-like. Skin lunged and my brother leapt back. But Skin kept pressing him with the hand that held his jacket. Walter jabbed again and Skin swept the blade away with his jacket, then kicked out his leg. Walter was hurt. He used his forearms to keep the knife off his body. Until, finally, he landed a kick on Skin, whose knife flew far from his body. Spotting an opening, Walter sent a volley of punches at Ale Skin's mug, knocking him down. Things had taken a turn again. My brother slammed Skin furiously into the ground.

The bouncer rushed in, pussyfooted behind Walter, hauled him up and clamped him. Ale sprung up. Knowing Walter couldn't shake the two of them off together, I scanned the room for help. But everybody was busy tussling. No one was free.

Now Ale Skin was the one caning my brother. Walter took punch after punch, one two, one two. He couldn't move, I couldn't watch. I spotted Ale Skin's blade. It wasn't far. I had to grab it, no matter what. I tried to get close, but a hard kick floored me. I couldn't move.

"Get her," I heard someone say.

I looked up and glimpsed the guy who'd punted me. Miseria and another chick rushed to tackle him. The guy stepped back and fell over me.

A hand swiped Skin's knife from right in front of my eyes, and brushed me. I knew that hand. I knew the arm that grabbed the man on top of me and heaved him up like a trash bag then slugged him, knocking him out.

It was my old man.

Realizing this, my breath caught in my throat.

My old man hid the knife and snuck up to where Walter was brawling. He body-slammed Ale Skin, forcing him to stop swinging and retreat. Shocked, the bouncer who held my brother loosened his grip enough for him to wriggle free.

"Out of the way, you old shit," said Ale Skin.

And my old man, fast like someone who knows how to move in shadow, pulled out the knife and drove it into his flesh.

I was numb.

As though the gray of the walls had infected us with something.

Inside was a shitshow. We headed toward the exit. None of us had got off scot-free, but we weren't too bruised up either. I was being shoved, swept away. I felt a hand on my waist. It was the old man. I didn't need to look to know it was him. Insults reached me like a dog's barking.

"This doesn't end here, motherfuckers!" screamed the skinheads we'd left behind.

Their voices wanted to pummel us. But they didn't follow. They stuck with Ale Skin.

I'm not sure how I knew that Ale Skin wouldn't make it out this time. No matter what they did, Ale Skin was as dead as Hernán.

I couldn't speak. Walter kept yelling and all I wanted was for him to shut up. For everybody to shut up and leave me alone with my brother. As always.

At some point, my old man let me go and stood there.

"We'll see each other again," Walter said.

Our old man said nothing, but relief shone in his eyes.

Twice I'd seen my old man kill.

Part Three

Part Three

Eartheater, the place where you learned to eat earth no longer exists. Everything will come crashing down," said Señorita Ana in my dream.

I looked around. I didn't know where we were. It wasn't my barrio, or the junkyard.

"What is this place?"

"I told you not to go back. That it wasn't allowed," Ana added. "Look at me now. They're coming for you. Will you keep on seeing?"

"No."

"What about me? What about everything you promised?"

"I don't want to anymore, Ana."

"But you could find them. Have them locked up. For me. They'll keep killing, out there. Don't you get it?"

Her voice was so horrifying I woke up.

Walter, what if we went away?"

I couldn't tell if he was asleep, but the moment he heard me he turned around and stuffed his head under a pillow. It made me happy to see him asleep in that bed. For a few minutes, it was like nothing had happened.

I waited. Listened to him breathing.

When I was about to leave, he said:

"Put the kettle on."

I turned on the burner, filled the kettle, set it on the stovetop, and stood watching the flame. My brother came in, opened the fridge, took out a bottle of water. He poured a glass and stood next to me, propped against the wall. He watched the flames as he drank.

"Remember when you forgot the old man's kettle and it went totally black? He wanted to kill you."

I watched the kettle till it clouded in my mind.

I didn't think I'd be so sad to leave.

Instead of answering, I asked:

"What about the bottles?"

Walter took another sip of water and said:

"The bottles stay."

We kept on watching the fire, in silence. Though I could tell the kettle was getting too hot, I didn't move. Walter turned off the burner, held the kettle under the faucet, and let a stream of water pour over it. Meanwhile, I grabbed the mate and the half-empty packet of yerba.

We sat at the table in the suite.

Not long after, Miseria shoved open the door and came in without knocking.

She glanced at the mate and sat down next to us. She was smiling differently.

"I can get some scratch from selling my bike. I'll bring the tools, though, they might come in handy," my brother said, as though it was just the two of us.

"I'm done with the earth," I said to Walter, who said nothing.

Miseria looked at me, wide-eyed.

I handed the mate to my brother, who passed it to her after filling it with water. Their fingers brushed.

"Where will we go?" I asked.

I don't know why but I wanted them to stop touching.

"I'm coming with you," Miseria cut in.

"Hell no. I don't want to end up behind bars," said Walter, and he slammed the mate on the table to show the conversation was over.

Miseria didn't scare. Instead, she grew bolder.

"I'll tell my ma I got a job. And come with you."

We looked at each other, Walter and me.

"What sort of jobs can you even do?" he said.

"Hell if I know. But she'll let me come with you if I tell her I got a job."

I said nothing but thought of how Miseria wasn't much older than I was when my old lady was killed. And that I liked the thought of her coming with us.

We were quiet for a long time. Then Miseria said:

"We'll take the mate," and laughed.

And I could tell Walter was crazy about her.

He got up and walked toward where I sat.

He kissed me on the forehead.

"Let's go, lil sis," he said.

Walter went somewhere with Miseria. Her house, I think. I didn't see them leave.

I lay down on my bed for a while. I was exhausted but wired and couldn't get to sleep. The worst combination. Not even my heart was resting. I shut my eyes.

What about Ezequiel? I wondered.

Ezequiel stays.

I had no one to talk to about it, so I asked and answered myself.

What about Ezequiel?

Ezequiel stays.

I opened my eyes and riffled through one of the drawers for a mirror. Mamá's. I thought of all the times I'd seen her look at herself in that mirror and tried to find some trace of her in it, something of Mamá's to help me in that moment.

I watched my lips moving.

Ezequiel stays.

I grabbed the blanket and pulled it over my head. I shut my eyes and cried.

Ezequiel was glad I'd asked to meet him.

I studied myself in the bathroom mirror and scanned my face for a change. Either there was nothing or I couldn't find it. Same old eyes.

I brushed my teeth. Applied mascara. Slung my backpack on. Fumbled for the keys, went outside, closed the door. As I was about to turn the key, I stopped. *Why bother lock up if we're leaving?* I left the door open. Tossed the keys in my bag and headed toward the precinct.

Ezequiel was at the entrance when I got there. I gave him a quick kiss. He wasn't angry I hadn't called. He asked if I wanted to go to his house and I said no, I'd rather drive around.

"Where?"

"Wherever. I need to talk," I said. But as soon as we got in the car, I fell quiet.

He said he wanted to get something to drink and I nodded. We pulled over to a grocery store run by some old woman. Ezequiel told me to choose whatever I wanted and I grabbed two beers from the fridge. All I cared was that they were cold. I flashed them at the woman and asked her for a packet of peanuts.

"I've got them by the kilo."

I asked her for a hundred grams.

Ezequiel didn't want beer. He asked her for three nips of something or other, and we left.

We drank for a while, stood on the pavement. Then Ezequiel said:

"Let's split."

We got in the car.

I set my half-empty beer between my feet and ate a fistful of peanuts to stave off a stomachache.

"Are you gonna tell me what's going on?"

"We're going away," I said, like that was all he needed to know.

Ezequiel went quiet as he drove. I waited for him to say something else.

"We're going away, Ezequiel, we're leaving the house."

"What for?"

"I can't deal with the people or the earth anymore."

He looked as if he hadn't heard me, just kept driving like it was nothing. Then he slowed down and turned into a dark, empty street.

"I'm done with dead people," I said.

Ezequiel pulled up to the curb and parked in front of a tree, his hand still on the steering wheel. I stared outside. I sipped on the beer again and again.

"Far?" Ezequiel asked.

"No clue."

I finished the beer, opened the door, got out, and tossed the bottle. I was trying to figure out how Ezequiel and me could carry on together, and it was all the same to me. Talking on the phone, texting. There was nothing I could say, nothing to comfort either of us.

I sat back in the car and looked over at him.

"We'll think of something."

I looked down. Ezequiel was quiet. He drank. I eyed the second beer.

"Take me to the cemetery?"

"The cemetery?"

I said yes, but that we should hit another shop first. We were gonna need a lot more booze.

We were off. Three of us. Three cell phones, three back-packs. Mine and Walter's were fit to burst. Miseria's was lankier than she was, like all she had in it was a pair of leggings.

We walked along the shoulder, the darkness shattered by the headlights of a truck barreling toward us. Another passed, then another. Nonstop trucks on the road. Their lights so strong they kept half-blinding us.

I could've asked Ezequiel to drive us but hadn't wanted to. The day before, I'd almost puked in his car. Besides, it would've been twice as hard to skip town.

I kept on walking, clutching my cell as though, from then on, Ezequiel would be held inside it.

We crossed an avenue that swelled into a river when it rained. I never used to like going there as a kid. I thought the gutters would swallow me up. The memory made me laugh.

Most of the houses were dark. Businesses were shuttered, as

usual. A cat peered through a broken window, eyeing us like it didn't give a shit.

The lights came and went with the trucks. There was hardly another soul around.

I thought of what Walter had said: "When we leave, we'll catch a bus or a train, or whatever comes our way."

We passed an abandoned gas station. It was huge, and I couldn't remember if I'd once seen it open or if it'd always been like that, boarded up with planks that hid the inside from view. Never any lights on. Whenever I went by there, I'd stand around and read the stuff scrawled on the wood. I'd memorized nearly every phrase. In a heart: "Yani & Lara 4ever." Beneath that: "Lucas, ur days r up." In black spray paint: "Power 2 Youth." Farther on, a stencil all around the barrio: "Melina dances in my lesbian heart." And scrawled across the wall, in huge letters: "Teen Respekt: Podestá is ur turf."

I skidded to a stop. Took a few steps back so I could see everything together: "Podestá is ur turf."

Before Walter sold his motorbike, Miseria asked him to teach her to ride. Walter had said no and Miseria had answered:

"I don't mean now. Out there, when you get another one."

Out there, like we were headed to China.

Miseria and Walter were almost a block ahead of me.

Alone, stopped in front of the gas station, I slipped off my shoes and pressed my feet into the earth. I pressed down hard and read the graffiti a couple more times. It was time to go.

I crouched, reached down. The earth was cold but pleasant: it was earth, not trash or dust. Earth from here. I grabbed a bit, clasped it in my hand. Would the earth know I'd been there?

I stood up and stuffed it in my pocket.

I slipped my shoes on again and hurried to catch up with Walter and Miseria.

We were outside, hanging on the shoulder.

Plenty of buses stopped around there and it wasn't late yet.

"Whatever comes first," my brother said, and we were all right with that.

We saw bus lights in the distance.

"Flag it down?" I asked.

Miseria smiled and shrugged like *what do I know*. But as the bus rolled closer, she raised her arm.

The bus stopped. We climbed in. It was practically empty. There was an old man asleep in his seat and, by the door, a couple making out. Nobody in the back. I pulled out three tickets, even though I didn't know where we were headed.

Walter and Miseria sat in the back, by the exit.

"I need the window seat," I said to Miseria.

She looked at me. I had the feeling she might make fun. But seeing how serious I was, she got up and moved over.

We were off.

Me at the window, Walter in the seat next to me, and Miseria sprawled with her head on my brother's shoulder.

The bus turned a corner, and I looked back at everything we were leaving behind us. There wasn't a soul around, and everything looked darker where we were going.

I thought to myself that I was alone, heading into a new place. The night kept some of it hidden and the lights revealed it little by little. I felt for the earth in my pocket. It wasn't much. The bus rattled over the pitted road. I put the earth in my mouth. I had nothing to wash it down with, but that was okay. I wanted to feel it.

I rested my head on the window, closed my eyes, and heard a voice lulling me to sleep.

"Eartheater, the place you learned to read the earth no longer exists."

A familiar-looking place gradually emerged in my head. My eyes adjusted, as though somebody had lit a candle. Walter, Miseria, and me sat on the sofa of the suite. We looked tired. Sad. We were older. A small boy darted around and I tried to track him with my eyes. He tripped. The doorway to my brother's room was walled over. The kid laid his hand on the bare bricks. The boy and the bricks were equally new and strange to me. Walter called the little tyke over, and he came running toward him and clambered onto him.

There were bottles in the suite, heaps of them.

"Eartheater, the place you learned to read the earth no longer exists," said the voice again, and I got angry.

My cell rang. I tried to answer but couldn't. I couldn't see the keypad or read anything. I thought that it might be Ezequiel, and felt nervous.

"They're waiting for you," Señorita Ana said, full of rage. "You've got work to do. It doesn't matter that the house is gone and only the suite is left. They're putting someone else in the earth."

I opened my eyes.

I thought of the day before, when Ezequiel went with me to Mamá's grave. I thought of the grave beside hers, of what it said on the tombstone. There was a bunch of stuff written on it. Mamá's had only a name and two dates.

I don't know who'd arranged for Mamá's gravestone. It hadn't been me. Nor Walter.

Gravestones, letters written to our dead.

Ana never got one.

Mamá got a name and two dates.

I glanced over. My brother held Miseria by the shoulders. They were both asleep.

I was thirsty for beer. The taste of earth still in my mouth, I took a deep breath but kept my eyes open. Through the bus window, I stared square into the night. I breathed out slow, thinking again of my old lady's grave, of the one next to it, of Ezequiel and me hitting the bottle like it was the end of the world.

"Ezequiel," I said. I thought of how I also wanted to have a name. Out there. One all my own.

ACKNOWLEDGMENTS

Thanks to Selva Almada and Julián López, for their excellent teaching.

To Marcelo Carnero and Victoria Schcolnik, who gave me Enjambre and in whose company I found that space to write for the first time. To all of my colleagues at the writing workshop and clinic, my first readers.

To Vera Giaconi, who helped me see even farther, and to write what I saw.

Thank you to my children, Ashanti, Ezequiel, Reina, Eva, Valentín, Ariadna, and Benja, for all the time we've had together.

ACKNOWLEDGMENTS

ABOUT THE AUTHOR

Dolores Reyes was born in Buenos Aires in 1978. She is a teacher, feminist, activist, and the mother of seven children. She studied classical literature at the University of Buenos Aires. *Eartheater* is her first novel.

A NOTE FROM THE TRANSLATOR

Eartheater is as much about story and character as it is about the language that shapes them—a mix of gritty, turf-bound slang and mysticism. The characters that populate these pages have a whiff of the Lost Boys and of the kids in *Lord of the Flies*. Either abandoned or let down by the grown-ups who were meant to protect them, they've been left to fend for themselves. They're also at odds with the other authority figures in the barrio, the cops—variously called yokes, cuffs, and pigs in this translation, adapted from the existing Spanish terms *yuta*, *ratis*, and *cana*—who have also let them down.

Out of this neglect rises our slovenly heroine, Eartheater, who will help solve the murders and missing persons cases that plague her community. Eartheater herself is terse and introverted, and there is a staccato rhythm to her no-nonsense worldview. She is hardboiled detective and bruja all rolled into one; tetchy teenager and wise seer wrapped in a single, waifish body. When she isn't busy reaching through darkness and time for the person she's seeking, she eats, listens to music, plays video games, drinks beer, hangs out with her brother, and fucks (a term she would use) her *yuta* boyfriend with relish.

Much like its heroine, *Eartheater* has also risen out of a particular moment and as a response to a particular neglect. Femicides remain widespread throughout Latin America and women have banded together in protest. (*Eartheater* is dedicated to two victims of femicide from the barrio where Dolores Reyes works as an activist and teacher.) Women authors continue to be overlooked on a national scale, and have joined forces to demand they be seen. We may have been aware of these things for a long time, but they are finally being addressed; even language is being righteously shaken and molded to make room for those it has long excluded.

In a way, the phrase *awante les pibis* serves as a snapshot of this groundswell. And though it occurs only once, I spent a good deal of time wrestling with it. In Argentina, *pibe* and *piba* mean "boy" and "girl," respectively; their plural forms are *pibes* and *pibas*. As is the case in many Romance languages, the masculine plural in Spanish is always used except when the grouping in question is entirely female (outrageous, we know). What's interesting about *pibis* is that it is gendered neither as male nor as female, but other. Meanwhile, *awante* is a distortion of the word *aguantar* ("wa" standing in for "gua"), which can mean to "endure" or "put up with" or "withstand," among other things, and is often used colloquially. A person who has *aguante*, for example, is someone with stamina. It is a phrase that in essence upends gendered grammar, both colloquially and off-handedly.

As it's used here—scrawled in Liquid Paper on the cover of a binder—*Awante les pibis* serves as an all-inclusive cry for solidarity. It's innocent, after a fashion, and yet illustrative of a deep desire for change on the part of the young people in the narrative. When translating this particular phrase, I tried to reach for something beyond the words that was both form-appropriate—Liquid Paper, binder—and context-appropriate—the kind of phrase you might see scrawled in a bathroom stall with a Sharpie. A phrase that perhaps once stood for something powerful. "Power 2 Youth" fit the bill. As best it could, anyway.

Something has been lost in this translation. Or rather, it was never there to begin with. English is not gendered in the same way as Spanish. On top of which, there is no English-language equivalent of the hyperlocal variant of Spanish in which *Earth-eater* was originally written: early twenty-first-century Argentinian Spanish from the outskirts of Buenos Aires. There is in fact no English-speaking Argentina, much less an English-speaking outskirts of an English-speaking place called Buenos Aires ("Good Airs"?).On the surface of things, this task—convincing you, the reader, that the work you have in your hands could have, in an alternate universe, been written in English by an English-speaking woman named Dolores Reyes ("Pains Kings"?)—may seem impossible. But the aim of literary translation is to convince you to suspend your disbelief, at least just long enough to make the impossible feel eminently plausible.

Julia Sanches

Here ends Dolores Reyes's
Eartheater.

The first edition of this book was printed and
bound at LSC Communications in
Harrisonburg, Virginia, August 2020.

A NOTE ON THE TYPE

The text of this novel was set in Granjon, an old-style
typeface designed by George W. Jones in the 1920s. Jones,
a British printer, drew inspiration from sixteenth-century
French punch-cutter and type designer Claude Gara-
mond's roman types and his contemporary Robert Granjon's italics to create this elegant, serif typeface. Granjon
became popular, as its delicate yet sure lines show up even
on smaller point sizes.

HARPERVIA

An imprint dedicated to publishing international voices,
offering readers a chance to encounter other lives and other
points of view via the language of the imagination.